a novel by

M.E. RHINES

SINK

ISBN 978-1-63422-239-6
Cover Design by: Marya Heiman
Typography by: Courtney Knight
Editing by: Cynthia Shepp

For more information about our content disclosure, please utilize the QR code above with your smart phone or visit us at
www.CleanTeenPublishing.com

To my very own Fawna, my sister Lindsey.

CHAPTER 1

It was the music that deceived me. The fraudulent melody that caught on the currents. Pleasing notes danced across every mermaid who twirled in tune with its harmonious offering. Its magic glided across the smooth, empty floor of the sunken ship we had claimed as our own, and then circled back to me. Each pluck of the guitar strings pulled me deeper into a trance of contentment.

Angelique strummed on the human instrument she'd recovered from another of their sunken vessels with suspicious expertise. As I watched the grace of her fingers, I couldn't help but wonder how we could possibly be sisters.

At eighteen, she was only two years older than me, but her body had a shape that would make a merman blush—if there were any left in the ocean. The deep brown locks of her hair swayed with the sea every time she bobbed her head to the music she created, and she smiled brightly at the attention her talent brought.

The laughter and innocent chatter surrounding me was enough to mask the treachery that was just ahead. It wasn't until I caught a glimpse of two great white sharks circling beneath the bow of the ship that dread snaked its way up my spine.

There was only one reason they would venture this far into the kingdom of Atargatis—someone had called them for a feeding.

I flicked my shimmering purple tail nervously at Mother, who turned to me with her coal-black eyes that burned into my flesh with a mixture of expectation and pride. We floated above the wheelhouse, our position providing us with a grand view of the entire celebration below.

She tilted her head toward me, nearly tipping off her elaborate, bejeweled crown. "Are you excited, Pauline?" Her voice was tender and maternal, with just a subtle hint of authority behind it—habit that came from years of being the matriarch.

"I want to be," I answered. Poseidon knew everyone else was. My worry had me far too distracted to enjoy the festivities. "What's going to happen?"

Mother brought an arm around me and pulled me close. "Just wait and see. This is the most exciting ritual in our culture, dear. It's what keeps our race going. I'm so pleased you're old enough to experience it with us."

I swallowed against my apprehension. Something dreadful was about to happen, I just knew it.

I moved my attention to the tiny sliver of light the sun cast down from above the waves, creating a perfect spotlight on our guest of honor—the human named Gene.

He held my oldest sister Fawna tightly against his side in the most loving, possessive way. His feet were planted firmly on the deck of what he called a *cargo ship*, which was recently lost to his people in a storm. Apparently, they used it to carry boxes of supplies from one patch of land to another.

Gill slits on both sides of his neck looked foreign on his skin. His flesh was darker than ours, kissed from the rays of the sun in a way we couldn't manage from the depths of the ocean. But then, all male hosts brought down here had the same alien look about them.

Fawna rubbed her swollen stomach as she spoke with various members of our clan. I couldn't hear them, but I knew what they were talking about just the same.

One mermaid would ask how the pregnancy was going; another would ask if her tail hurt from the extra weight. Fawna would smile and claim that everything was just perfect, even though everyone heard her daily spells of morning sickness.

They would ask her the baby's name and ponder the color of her tail. The same sort of meaningless questions that came around every time a mermaid was with child. The one question no one ever seemed to ask, though, was where the human father disappeared to just before birth.

"Here," Mother said as she handed me a plate of sliced black-and-white flesh. "A special meal for our guest of honor. And you, my dear Pauline, get the privilege of delivering it to him."

I gasped. "Beaked Sea Snake?" The poison inside this snake's meat was paralyzing. So potent that we only ate it if we were undergoing a massive medical procedure, and then the toxins were filtered out through the gills. "Is Gene sick?"

"Of course he's sick, darling. He's a human. Humans are filled with parasites and germs. There's bound to be something crawling about in his body."

I twisted a jet-black curl of hair around my finger. "Will he be all right?"

"Of course. His body is used to the invaders by now."

"Then why— "

"It's part of the ritual, Pauline. You are the youngest in attendance, which means you must deliver Gene his fate."

"His fate?"

"That's right." Her words were cold, frigid even. So detached I might've thought she meant—

No. Impossible. Gene's gills worked the same way as a mermaid's. They would filter out the toxins.

So then...

"What *is* his fate?"

She pressed her lips together in a tight, impatient line. "You'll see soon enough."

The defiant side of me burned to ask her who we were to decide his fate. I knew better, though. No one argued with Queen Calypso unless they wished banishment upon themselves. It would be foolish to think she might offer me some leniency based on a shared bloodline.

Mother knew no mercy.

So, I offered a slow, obedient nod and set my sights on Gene. The few feet I swam to reach him felt like an eternity, but when I approached, he released my sister and took me in his arms instead. A warm,

SINK

welcoming hug straight from the heart of a happy, carefree friend.

"My favorite sister," he murmured into my hair.

My heart started to swell, but I squelched the feeling and pulled away. "How are you, brother?"

"Such a party! And all for me. It's magnificent."

I shook my head, amazed at the progress he'd made. Only months ago, this lonely, bitter sailor was lured into the depths by way of my sister's song. He swore to Fawna, and to me, that he would never forgive our clan for turning him into a monster. The gills gifted to him by Fawna's kiss branded him a beast in his eyes.

It didn't take long for him to change his tune. Once he'd realized he was the only male among dozens of females, and how important that made him, the transition happened quickly. All the mermaids wanted him, but he was tethered to a royal. What better mate could there be?

Fawna's silver eyes flitted to the plate in my hand before she regarded me with a sly, knowing smile.

"What have you got there?" she asked with a gleam in her eye.

"Um..." I stumbled, searching for the right answer. My gut told me Mother wouldn't want me to reveal the side effects of the Beaked Sea Snake. My conscience fought hard to send the truth to my lips, but my submission won out. "It's a special snack. For Gene."

Gene's smile reached his eyes. "It looks delicious. Did you make it?"

"No!" My answer was too loud, too quick. I didn't

want any association with whatever deed was about to be done.

He arched a brow at me, and then laughed.

"Forgive me, Princess Pauline. I didn't mean to imply that a royal would work in the kitchen."

Panic grabbed at my throat, choking my words back.

"Don't mind her, dearest," Fawna said, drawing his attention from me. "Pauline hasn't been feeling well today. She isn't herself."

"Nothing serious, I hope."

I shook my head.

"A touch of wave sickness, I think," Fawna offered on my behalf. "She's always been sensitive to the ocean's movements."

Lying was one of her many gifts, and she told the story without a hitch. It was a talent passed down from Mother. One I did not possess.

"Looks like you were born in the wrong terrain."

I managed a weak smile as I held the plate out to him. He took it, and I swam as fast as I could back to Mother.

"Now what?" I asked her between heavy breaths.

"Now we wait. And no matter what happens, Pauline, you must not intervene. Do you understand?"

My eyes widened, my heart hammering against my rib cage. A fear I didn't understand tugged at my tailfin, making it feel like an anchor had been tied to its end. I sank against the wall of our pirated vessel and watched the chaos as it unfolded in slow motion.

Gene laughed at something my sister said just before it hit him. His smile fell in an instant as soon as the sudden deadening feeling pummeled into his chest. He dropped the plate and held out his hand. From my experience with Beaked Sea Snake, he was seeing double the fingers.

A fogginess washed over his eyes. He reached out for Fawna for just a second before his arms fell to his sides, limp and useless. Then, his human legs gave out from under him. A loud crack sounded as his knees made impact with the hard floor of the ship.

When he finally fell backward, my sister stood over his paralyzed body with a shameless, cruel smirk that gave me the chills. My mother, hovering well above me, nodded her approval with a warm, glowing pride showing on her face.

I looked around, expecting to see the same shocked expression I wore among my clan. But not one jaw was dropped. Every one of them watched with tense, excited eyes. They looked like blood-thirsty demons from where I was sitting.

"Mother," I whispered. "What's going on?"

She didn't hear me.

"My Queen," someone shouted from below. "What are your orders?"

Mother took in a long, powerful breath and shouted, "Air him out."

I gasped, disbelief shuddering through me. "Mother," I screamed. "Mother, you can't!"

My protests were drowned out by the unified battle cry that erupted from every member of our clan. Angelique dropped her guitar, dashing for Gene with two other mermaids close behind.

I rushed for him, but Mother grabbed my arm

with bruising fingers.

"Let me go," I demanded.

Even through the screeching cheers below, I could hear Mother's teeth grinding. "Don't make a scene."

I stilled, having every intention to stay put and comply, as usual. But then, I caught a glimpse of Gene's face. While his muscles were tight and immobile, his eyes were filled with a conscious terror. They pleaded with me from across the ship, begging me to save him.

Before I could stop myself, I twisted my arm out of Mother's grasp and swam to him, hoping to talk some sense into my sister before she did something terrible.

It was no use. I couldn't reach them. They had too much of a head start. All I could do was watch as they snatched the helpless human and dragged his lifeless body up, up, and up until...

Bubbles sprayed all around them as they held Gene's head and neck above water, but kept their own gills safely submerged. Even if he had working legs to thrash and fight with, he would be outmatched. Our tails treaded water in a way a human's boney appendages couldn't come close to.

He was in our world, by no choice of his own. We brought him down here against his will, and now that he was a part of it, my mother was sending him back home to die.

The gills would not disappear. They would only struggle for a short while before giving up to the heat of the land above. Gene's chest moved in and out, in

SINK

faster but shallower spurts.

I kicked my tail harder. Just as he came into my reach, he took one final gulp of air from his own world, and the movement stopped.

Mother had killed him.

CHAPTER 2

"Stop making up stories." Sapphire pools of skepticism gawked at me in disbelief. My best friend Jewel floated in front of me, silently imploring me to admit jest.

I shushed her and inclined my head toward our powers instructor, Ms. Star.

"Why?" she asked. "Afraid she'll pull your tail out from under your little joke?"

My face burned red. "I'm not lying."

"I didn't say you were *lying*, sheesh. Don't get so upset."

"How else do you explain where all the human males have gone?"

"Um, I don't know." Jewel raised her shoulders in a disinterested shrug. "Maybe they just go home when they're done."

I shook my head. How could she be so naïve? "You'll be sixteen soon," I reminded her. "They'll let you attend the next merling shower when you are. You'll see it's true."

Jewel bit her lip, running her eyes along my face. She was trying to use her telepathy to read my mind, a power not many mermaids, including myself, could master. It was no trouble for her, though.

SINK

She had it figured out by the time she was ten.

"Stop doing that," I complained. "It's totally an invasion of privacy. Not cool."

"Sorry." She blushed, leaning in to whisper, "So, they're actually killing them?"

"Yes! Good Poseidon, that's what I've been telling you."

"Am I interrupting your conversation, ladies?" Ms. Star wiggled her way between us.

I straightened my spine and lowered my eyes. "Of course not, Ms. Star. I'm sorry for being rude."

Jewel smooshed her lips together, blowing air kisses in my direction. Ever the rebellious one, her nickname for me was *kiss-up*. She always said I needed to loosen up, break a few rules, and have some fun.

Easy for her to say. She didn't have the murderous Queen Calypso for her mother.

"You, of all my students, should be paying attention, Pauline."

I winced. "Yes, ma'am."

"You're the only one left who hasn't discovered her natural gift."

"I understand, Ms. Star."

"And you're the oldest one in my class."

I rubbed my temples. "I'm trying."

"You won't be able to take your place next to your mother if you don't find it."

"Hey!" Jewel's cheeks puffed up as she pushed me out of the line of fire, planting herself in front of Ms. Star instead. "She gets it, okay? She's doing her best. You bullying her isn't going to help things."

Ms. Star pressed her lips into a tight line. "I'm not *bullying* her, Jewel. I'm *teaching* her."

"No, you're making her feel awful about herself."

"My methods are not up for dis—"

"I'm certain Queen Calypso wouldn't be at all happy about the way you're addressing the princess."

The instructor's eyes softened as she looked behind Jewel to me, along with every young mermaid in the class. My tail wobbled under me. I wanted to shrink away and disappear. If I could swim away and hide, I would have. But our kingdom was small, and there was nowhere to go but home.

Frankly, after seeing what my family was capable of, I'd rather be here.

"Pay attention, won't you?" Ms. Star asked, her tone now easy and compliant.

"Of course."

With one hard swish of her tail, she propelled herself back to the front of the class. One by one, each set of eyes that were on me followed her direction.

"Now..." She cleared her throat, collecting herself. "We have covered the first three talents over the last few weeks. Let's review, shall we?"

Jewel groaned, boredom choking the sound from her throat.

Ms. Star ignored her. "Of course, there is the ever-dying power of telepathy. Not many mermaids will be dealt this type of faculty, but it will certainly come in useful for you, Jewel."

Jewel swam in place just ahead of me. Her shoulders bobbed at the mention of her talent, as if it was nothing at all. What I wouldn't give to be more like her.

She was gifted, bold, and not scared of anything or anyone. To top it off, she had the most beautiful aqua-blue hair of all the mermaids in our clan. She kept it restrained in a tight braid, so it wouldn't get in her way. If it were mine, I would let it float free and wild.

But it wasn't. I was stuck with this jet-black hair that stuck out like a rusted anchor. Didn't matter what I did with it. Between it, my violet eyes, and matching tail, I was the most colorful fish in the ocean, when all I wanted was to blend in.

"Makes it easy to know when someone is lying," Jewel offered.

"It also requires a great deal of restraint. You don't have the right to go around dipping into a mermaid's private thoughts, remember that. You are only to act according to the queen's command."

Jewel rolled her eyes, but acknowledged the order with a nod. Even she knew her gift needed much discipline.

"Sorcery is, of course, forbidden," Ms. Star said. "Although it is something each of us is capable of, you'll steer clear of it unless you wish to end up like Myrtle, the banished sea witch."

"Ms. Star." A redheaded girl raised her hand. "Why are we skilled with a tool that we can't use?"

"Sorcery is dangerous. It gives a mermaid the illusion of power and control, but those two traits must only be exercised by Her Majesty."

I sighed. Mother had outlawed sorcery as another means of controlling her subjects, nothing more.

Ms. Star went on. "Precognition. A fancy talent, isn't it? And if you've mastered it well enough, you could earn yourself a seat at Queen Calypso's royal table." She moved her attention to a young mermaid in the front of the class. One who recently discovered that seeing the future was a gift she possessed. "Wouldn't that be something, Ariana?"

The merling couldn't have been more than twelve. Her eyes lit up with excitement as she moved her head up and down lightning fast. "Yes, Ms. Star. I would love that."

"Tell us, have you had any new visions? I'm always fascinated to hear."

"Um…" The girl shrunk back. "I don't want to say."

"Oh, come on now. Give us a peek into that beautiful mind."

"I-I have been dreaming about fire."

"Fire? You mean on a ship above us? Maybe we'll receive a new batch of sailors then, eh?" Ms. Star winked, but Ariana returned her enthusiasm with a deep-set frown.

"The fire was at the palace."

The instructor stared for a moment before chuckling. "Impossible. Fire cannot survive under water. It requires the human's air to grow. What you've been having are dreams, nightmares. Nothing more."

Ariana glanced back at me, causing the hair on my arms to stand. "I'm sure you're right, Ms. Star."

"Let's move on to the last, but perhaps the most

important, power of all," Ms. Star continued. "Hypnosis. Without it, our existence would not be possible."

My fingers curled into my palms, the sting of my nails keeping me distracted enough to prevent an outburst.

Hypnosis. It was just a means to murder in the guise of procreation.

"Not every mermaid is destined to find a human mate, but for those who are, perfecting this craft is crucial to all of us as a whole."

Bouts of giggles erupted from a few of the other girls.

"Once you have found the human the ocean deems you tied to, your song will come forth without effort. If your instrument is not properly tuned, however, the gift will be wasted. Your human will not be drawn to you, and you'll have lost your chance to contribute to the clan. That isn't an acceptable option, is it, girls?"

In unison, the class responded, "No, Ms. Star."

"So, come now, let's practice."

The class sucked in a collective breath and released musical notes, one by one. Even though they had all found their primary talents, it was not uncommon to find hypnosis as a secondary endowment.

While they looked to perfect a second ability, I hadn't managed to find my first. As frightened as I was at the idea of having no gift bestowed to me at all, I would not seek this one out. I would take no part in the massive slaughter.

As the others sang their prompted melodies, my

mouth stayed clenched shut.

Ms. Star raised a brow in my direction, and then signaled to the class for silence. "Is something wrong with your throat, Pauline?"

I shook my head, but offered no further explanation.

"Why are you not singing with us?"

I didn't answer. Defiance was not in my character, and I had no idea how to vocalize it.

"She's probably worried she has *The Voice*," Jewel offered.

Ms. Star scrunched her nose at the notion. "I should think that would please you after all your searching. Wouldn't it be grand if all this time, hypnosis was your paying feature?"

"She says we're killing the humans after we've... used them. Pauline said she saw it with her own eyes at Fawna's merling shower."

Our teacher's hand flew to cover her gaping mouth as a few of the girls in the class shrieked. "Pauline," she said through parted fingers. "What were you thinking telling the merlings such a story?"

"It isn't a story!" Somewhere, deep in the pit of my belly, I found my voice. It was timid and shrill, but present. And I was going to use it. "You know it's true, Ms. Star. You know it because you were there, too."

She floated a few inches back, no doubt stunned by my explosion. "You know what is done at those events are not to be discussed with the children. I'm certain it was explained to you as a condition of your attendance."

"They deserve to know what you're training them to do, don't they?"

"Where is this insubordination coming from? You're usually such a quiet young mermaid. Usually so—"

"Polite?" I interrupted. "Gracious? I know. I'm the obedient little princess who always does what's right. This is no different. I'm trying to do what's good."

"You think by traumatizing these girls, you're doing what's *good*?"

"I think by telling them the truth I am, yes."

"Forgive me, Princess, but I believe the queen will have a different opinion on the matter."

I blanched. My face tingled as the blood drained from it. Mother will air me out alive for this.

CHAPTER 3

Even as my skin burned, I had to admire the queen's creativity. My muscles ached from being forced into the fetal position for so long. The clam Mother locked me inside was giant by bivalve standards, but it still made for cramped quarters.

The darkness drank me in as if I were a cocktail made from the finest of seaweed. In any other circumstance, the quiet and stillness would be welcomed. Perhaps I could even stomach the foul-smelling bile the creature excreted if it meant some time in solitude. I was content with my own company. In fact, I preferred it.

It was my allergy to shellfish that made this punishment so menacing. I didn't need to see them to know painful blisters formed on my skin every minute. By the time she let me out, my flesh would no doubt look like I had taken a swim through a bloom of jellyfish.

That was, *if* she let me out. Maybe she would leave me in here for eternity to rot as my body attacked itself for days until...

No. Even Queen Calypso wasn't so wicked that she would do such a thing to her own daughter. Exile me like Myrtle, sure. Murder me? At least, I *hoped* she wasn't capable of such a thing.

Still, I wasn't sure how much longer I could stand being so itchy and prickly. As I had already attempted a dozen times, I felt my way to the small slit near the clam's opening and tried to wiggle my fingertips between the two shells to pry them open. It was no use. This thing wasn't opening his jaws until Mother commanded him to.

Out of pure frustration, I banged my fist against my captor's hard armor. "Sheep fish," I snapped at it. "Why don't you think for yourself for once and open up because you know it's right?"

The slimy center of the thing gurgled underneath me, as if to shush me up, and then his noise stopped all of a sudden. A woman's voice, muffled and stifled by the barrier between us, said something. At the words, the clam released its tight hold, allowing his shell to open just a crack.

I wanted to lunge for fresh air. To rinse my skin of the substance that stung it like a hundred jabs from a lionfish. Knowing it must be my mother on the other side made staying in my safe, albeit painful, pen a tempting option.

"Come on out." Relief swelled in my chest when I recognized Angelique's softer voice, not Mother's.

Still, the idea that Mother could be in my sister's company kept me hidden. "Why have you come for me?"

"We need to have a talk."

"Is Mother with you?"

"No, little one. It's only me"

"I think I should continue with the queen's punishment," I said. "I'd rather not risk upsetting her further by skipping out early."

"Mother knows I'm here, Pauline. She won't be cross."

I stuck my head out of the clam's opening just enough to look around. From the best I could tell, Angelique was indeed alone. The grotto used as a prison was small, making it easy to get a good view of everything but behind me.

Just to be sure, I asked, "Do you swear it?"

Angelique flashed me a humored grin and said, "I promise."

The clam's upper shell was heavy, and Angelique made no move to help me lift it. When I finally managed to get out, I turned to my sister to find her face contorted in horrified displeasure.

"What's the matter?" I asked.

She covered her mouth, stifling back a gag. "I'm glad I brought this." Angelique raised a purple bottle with a squeeze ball dangling from the top of it.

I stretched my arms out to survey the damage. Pus-filled bubbles canvased my body from head to tail. Only my breasts were spared, since a thick shell bikini top covered them.

"Come with me." Angelique swam to a long, flat rock and sat on it. I stayed in place, and she rolled her eyes at my hesitation. "Good Poseidon, Pauline. I'm not going to bite. I haven't turned into our mother just yet."

I drew my bottom lip between my teeth and made a slow approach. She pulled me to sit next to her, and then squirted my arms with whatever was inside the bottle. A cold sensation coated my skin, ceasing the burning on contact.

A long, forceful breath left my chest. So much better.

When she moved to apply the mystery liquid to my tail, I asked, "Is it magic?"

Her eyes flew to my face. "Of course not. It's medicine."

"Oh. I'm sorry."

"That's all right. It's difficult to tell the difference sometimes, I suppose."

"Thank you."

She spritzed the last of my blisters before setting the bottle down. "I'm supposed to chastise you, you know."

"I suspected as much." Guilt should be dancing in my stomach like a water bug. I felt none, but that lack of remorse filled me to my eyeballs with shame.

Angelique leaned in, her tawny curls brushing against my shoulder. "We have these rules in place for good reason. You shouldn't have told those girls about the ceremony."

"I only told Jewel."

"You know Jewel well enough to know she can't keep a secret. She's a blabbermouth."

That was true. Jewel drooled over gossip and was downright addicted to spreading it. Maybe my subconscious was hoping she would tell everyone. Perhaps deep down, I wanted her to do my dirty work for me.

"We shouldn't be doing it at all," I fumed.

"How else are we supposed to continue our race? The mermen are gone; they're never coming back. This is the only way."

"Murdering them when we're through does nothing to aide our cause. In fact, I should think it hinders it."

"And how is that?" Angelique wrinkled her nose at me.

"If we kept them alive, we could have more merlings, couldn't we? Fawna could have five of them instead of one. Now that we've killed him off, we have to wait until the next ship sinks to find another male to mate with, and then hope the ocean matches his soul to one of our mermaids."

She shook her head. "We must ensure genetic diversity."

"Don't be so naïve, Angelique." I placed a hand on her shoulder, and then lowered my voice. "This has nothing to do with guaranteeing different-colored tails and eyes. Mother has them killed to exercise power."

My sister's brown eyes widened, and she squeaked, "To say such a thing is treason. What has gotten into you?"

"What we're doing is *wrong*. I can't pretend it isn't happening. This time, I can't be Mother's good little girl."

"It isn't wrong. We're doing the earth a favor by ridding it of as many of those vile creatures as possible." She ran a finger along a line of puckered skin on my shoulder. "Pauline, you, of all people, should know how awful they are."

"It was a fish hook. They weren't hunting mermaids. I just happened to be in the wrong place at the wrong time. Besides, how can we claim to be so much better than they are when we're luring them to their deaths in such a way? It's barbaric... It's evil... It's downright human by your standards!"

Angelique pressed her lips into a tight, flat line of frustration. "There's obviously no talking you into thinking with a rational mind."

"I suppose we'll just have to disagree on the definition of rational."

"Your estimation on it makes no difference." She moved from the rock and swam a few feet away. "The only mermaid's opinion that does matter is the queen's. She wishes to see you in her throne room."

As if I were a common peasant, I floated in line behind the other mermaids, who all waited for their short moment with the queen. That was fine by me, since each of us awaited sentencing. Each accused of acting against the queen in some manner.

Mother's palace was magnificent and elaborate. Bright, sparkling jewels decorated the walls, which were built from the most colorful corals. I fixed my line of sight on the large, red stone hung just above Her Majesty's throne. A ruby, one of the human visitors once told me it was called. The color of blood and power. No wonder it was Queen Calypso's favorite.

Angelique pinched my arm, and I elbowed her

back. "Hey!"

"The line is moving." She waved ahead of us. "Swim forward."

I swished my tail enough to bump me up a couple of inches. "I'm sorry. I hadn't noticed."

"Too busy daydreaming, no doubt. Quite like you, little one."

Little one. Angelique's pet name for me since I was a tiny merling. Now, as a full-fledged mermaid, the cutsie nickname made me cringe. The words came off too condescending, too informal, for my age. As if she thought herself so superior to me, she couldn't be bothered to address me properly. Of course, I would never say anything. She meant no harm by it; habit was all it was.

Taking a deep breath, I scanned the room for something else to keep my mind off the wrath Mother was preparing to cast at me. One single mermaid clutching onto her merling for dear life floated between my humiliation and me.

Her smiling little infant pointed at the tiara set atop Angelique's head, but my sister paid the girl no mind. The sparkling gemstones made up a smaller version of the crown the queen wore even in her sleep. A symbol of authority and prestige, one that I refused to put on.

I thought myself no better than the other mermaids in our kingdom. That royal blood rushed through my veins made no difference to me.

Queen Calypso waved the other mermaid toward her, pretending not to notice her own daughter was next in line.

She addressed the woman, who still held her child tight against her chest. "Abigail, you have been accused of stealing from the palace garden. What have you to say for yourself?"

The woman's head fell, and a shimmering tear floated up from her cheek to disperse into the salty ocean waters. "I won't deny it, Your Majesty. My little Leah was starving and—"

"Are the provisions I provide you not sufficient?" Queen Calypso's face remained as hard as stone. Not a speck of emotion could be found in her eyes, nor did a single muscle twitch to reveal an ounce of sympathy for the woman's plight.

"Of course. You're quite generous in what you offer us. But, I'm afraid someone stole everything from my grotto—including all our food. We were ransacked. Everything is gone."

"Why did you not report this to one of my guards?"

"I did, Your Majesty. To your first in command. A report was filed, but my baby... she still needs to eat."

The queen brought her fingers together to a steeple, placed them under her chin, and said, "And so you thought it a good idea to resolve your predicament by stealing from me?"

"I couldn't watch my daughter starve." Her voice cracked, and she kissed the top of the merling's head.

"Actually, Abigail, that's exactly what you'll do."

I gasped, loud enough to draw a glare from Mother.

"No provisions for you or your daughter for one week."

"Oh please, Queen Calypso." The woman fell to

her knees, her body trembling. "I will gladly go without and accept my penalty. But, please, don't punish my daughter for my crime."

"Consider it a learning opportunity, peasant. Your young merling will figure out early in life what happens when you act against me."

"No. No, please." Desperation strained the woman's voice, pinching my stomach into a knot of pity.

"Another word and I'll make it two weeks."

The woman stilled, sniffled, and then nodded.

Any attempt I had ever made at telepathy always fell flat, but I had to give her some hope.

Don't worry, I thought. *I'll bring food to you and your baby.*

Abigail swung around and swam for the exit, pausing half a second to lock eyes with me. She heard it. The softened look on her face, aglow with gratitude, thanked me when she couldn't use her words.

You're a saint. The tiny, quiet words whispered somewhere deep inside my mind.

"Angelique." Mother's voice boomed and echoed. "Take the others and leave me with Pauline. I'll grant them their trials tomorrow."

My sister took my hand in hers, giving it a gentle squeeze, before she bowed and took her leave.

CHAPTER 4

Tension crackled between us, leaving the air thick and muggy. We watched each other, both stubborn and silent until Mother snickered. "You look like a red fish."

I gave her a nervous giggle. "All thanks to your creativeness, My Queen."

"Yes." Her mouth lifted into a self-satisfied smile. "It was an ingenious method of discipline, if I might say so myself."

"One that will no doubt go down in the record logs."

"My, Pauline. You wouldn't be trying to win me over with flattery, would you?"

"I suppose I thought it wouldn't hurt under the circumstances."

"It most certainly *could* hurt. There isn't much I despise more than false compliments."

I winced and said, "I'm sorry, Your Majesty."

Mother leaned forward, drawing her eyebrows down and squinting her eyes to measure me. "Why did you do it, Pauline? After I instructed you in no uncertain terms to keep the happenings of the festival to yourself, why would you tell the merlings?"

"It was the right thing to do." I licked my lips and

took in a tight breath. "Why did you do it, Mother? He was innocent."

The queen rose from her throne, straightening her tiara and setting it deeper into her sheen of silver hair. "None of them are innocent. Have I not spent your life telling you as much? Humans are wicked. Infected with immortality down to their core. Gene was no different."

"Did you kill my father, as well?" I blinked back the burn that seethed behind my eyes. It was a question I knew the answer to, but I had to hear it from her nonetheless.

A malicious laugh bubbled up from the pit of her stomach. "Your *father*? You've gone mad, child. You haven't got a father. None of the mermaids do anymore."

"You did, then."

"Yes, Pauline." She swayed closer to me with her lips puckered out in a pretend pout. "Your genetic donor suffered the exact same fate as Gene. Although, he put up a bit more of a fight. Quite impressive, if I'm honest."

"You're a monster."

She raised a hand, preparing to slap it down, when the floor beneath us jolted to a heavy rumble. Her eyes lit brightly at the quake, a sincere, thrilling happiness taking over her expression.

My stomach plummeted down to the bottom of my gut.

Not again.

"It seems, my dearest daughter, you have not learned your lesson." She spoke over the deafening screech descending on us. "And I believe I've found a most fitting punishment."

The double doors to the throne room swung open. Fawna, Angelique, and Prawn, Mother's first in command, rushed in. Not for the first time, I thought just how appropriate the officer's name was.

With her pointy nose, buggy eyes, and pale pink tale, she did, in fact, resemble a prawn, perhaps more so than a mermaid. A dreadful odor of decaying fish guts followed her around, the way it always did. Terrible teeth, Mother said, rotting from the gums up. I wasn't so convinced. Knowing how cruel she could be, a decomposing soul was my guess.

"My Queen." The guard hurried to bow before continuing. "All untainted mermaids have assembled in the square."

Untainted, meaning those who had not already had a human mate.

Fawna swam back toward the door. "Mother, the ship is coming down fast. We should hurry if we are to reach any survivors."

"Not you, Princess Fawna." Prawn squared her shoulders and waved at my sister's stomach. "Your condition is too far along. Forgive me, but the excitement might bring about labor."

"You want me to miss the hunt?"

"It's for the best."

"Agreed," Mother and Angelique said in unison.

"But... I haven't missed a hunt since I was sixteen years old."

Angelique rubbed our eldest sister's stomach, affection evident in every stroke. "You'll help with the next one." She moved her gaze toward me, her eyes squinting with contempt. "This time, you can help by keeping an eye on Pauline until we're through."

Heat burned on my cheeks. As if, at sixteen, I required a merling-sitter.

"Pauline will be joining you on the hunt." Mother's announcement made all of us jump.

Blood pulsed in my ears, and the room started to spin. "You can't expect me to watch this."

"Not at all. I expect you to give your clan your participation. Prawn, provide my daughter with a spear. She will be the one to kill the first human who doesn't react to our song."

Prawn clenched her jaw, but nodded as she shoved the spear she held into my hand. "Of course. Come with me, Princess."

"Mother..." I shook my head. "I can't do this."

The queen's black eyes stared at me, her right eyebrow lifted, daring me to go against her wishes. As usual, she had twisted her matronly hair tight in a bun in the center of her crown, revealing the bulging tendons on her slender neck. They flexed as she addressed me, her voice lacking even the most basic softness that should accompany motherhood. Queen Calypso was a gruesome, iron-fisted ruler, incapable of being anything different.

"You will do as I say, or I swear to Poseidon, you will end up just like your aunt Myrtle."

I gasped, but I was alone in my surprise. What seemed to be common knowledge to the rest smashed into me as if one of the human's anchors fell on my body. "*Aunt* Myrtle?"

"I *will* exile you, child. If I could do it to my own sister, don't think for a moment I wouldn't do it to you."

My lips trembled, holding back words that would only come out a jumbled mess, anyway. The terrible sorceress my mother villainized during my bedtime stories was my... aunt? Cast out for what? It didn't matter before, but the truth meant everything now that I knew she shared my blood.

There would be time for answers later. Now, I needed a way out of this slaughter.

Mesmerized by the sharp tip of the instrument of death in my hands, my mind braided together a plan. As Mother wished, I would accompany the clan to the sinking vessel. When the others zeroed in on their prey, minds drunk with blood lust and the unquenchable thirst to find the next mate, I would sneak away, reveal myself to the humans, and lure them away from the ambush.

"Okay," I said, swallowing hard against my deceit. "I'll help."

Prawn swooshed her tail hard. "All right, then. Let's move!"

A wall of bubbles erupted as Angelique followed her lead, leaving Fawna and Mother behind. I lingered just long enough to flash them an uncertain glance before I joined the clan outside.

The seafloor came alive with battle cries and screams, and, in the blink of an eye, I was part of a scene I generally watched from the safety of the palace.

So, this is what it means to no longer be a mer-

ling, I thought.

One thing I knew for certain, I would take Mother up on her offer of banishment before I became one of them.

The creak of breaking steel and crumbling wood came from just overhead. Moving together like a school of silverfish, a dozen mermaids shot for the surface. I trailed behind, just far enough to the right to keep a bit of open ocean between us. As the light of the land came into view, so did the vessel, already well underwater.

Mermaids assaulted the fishing boat, darting between nets and into the wheelhouse window, singing their songs of seduction as they went. Each one would emerge snarling like sharks when their search yielded no humans. Scanning the murky water, I caught sight of a large, circular shadow floating above us. *A life raft.* I had to get them away before the others noticed.

I flicked my tail with as much force as I could, but, before I could regain control of my direction, I swam right into a tangled mess of seaweed. As I tugged at the vegetation, I collided with something hard, bruising my shoulder. Whatever I had made impact with weaved itself around my torso. With blind hands, I felt the solid mass, the distinctive shape turning my blood to ice.

A sickening, petrified scream left my lips, piercing the water surrounding me. My gills sucked in extra liquid, trying to spread more oxygen throughout my body to keep me from passing out.

It was a human. *A human.*

And instead of swimming away in fright the way a normal human should, it pressed into me harder. Each brush of the current barreled him into me again and again.

Once I managed to rip the seaweed off my face, giving me a better view, my stomach roiled. It wasn't just a human touching me—it was a *dead* human. I shoved the corpse away from me, suddenly feeling as if sea-lice crawled over every inch of my skin.

A shudder jolted through my body at the sight of him. His face had only just began expanding with waterlog, but his dark eyes viewed me with a creepy lifelessness that made me want to vomit.

"What are you waiting for?" Prawn and the others watched me from a distance with expectation, and she waved at the spear in my hand. "Gut him."

The way she glared at the human told me she thought he was still alive. As disgusted as I was at the prospect of injuring him, dead or not, it might be just enough distraction to get them off my back long enough to lead the other sailors to safety.

A bitter bile rose in my throat. I swallowed it down, determined to use the poor man's fate to my advantage. To the advantage of all his crewmen who were still alive.

"Poseidon help me," I whispered as I lunged forward, thrusting the triangular tip into his belly. The waves pushed him forward, giving the illusion that he doubled over in pain. Because death had already claimed him, the blood only flowed out instead of gushing as it would have had his heart still been beating. I held my breath, praying my scrutinizing audience wouldn't catch on.

Prawn nodded her approval, too consumed by her mission to notice how little he bled. "Congratulations, Princess. Your mother will be pleased."

I blinked at her. Remorse and disgrace rattled through me. It didn't matter that I hadn't killed him; I *had* mutilated his body. The feeling of that weapon piercing his flesh would haunt me the rest of my days.

"Retrieve your spear," she ordered. "You may need it again. Ladies, continue your search. Sing for survivors."

The second they turned their attention back to the hunt, I took off again for the lifeboat. A shadow still bobbled on the surface. I came out just north of the humans, making sure to appear in the same direction the surf would take them.

I sucked in a gill-full of water, and then crashed through the surface. My eyes would take some time to adjust to the brighter conditions of the dry world. Green spots covered three lumpy silhouettes squished together in the boat. As I squinted at them to focus their features, they clearly saw me just fine.

"What is it?" a female's voice shrieked.

The unsteady voice of an older man stuttered. "I-I think it's a girl."

"A girl in the middle of the ocean?" the woman taunted. "Don't be stupid."

"Well she's certainly not a fish!"

I couldn't help but giggle as they squabbled and tried to determine my species. Just to add to the nonsense, and to entice them enough to follow, I flipped my tail up behind me and dove back under the water, then emerged again with a wave in the direction opposite my clan.

"I think she wants us to follow her," a third voice, male but less masculine, suggested.

"That means we go the other way," his female counterpart insisted, her teeth chattering as shock set in.

No. She may have just been through a terrible tragedy, one that might keep her away from the ocean forever, but for what I was risking, she would listen. They all would. I smacked the foot of my tail down on the surface of the water with a *crack*. My oxygen was running out; shouting at them to stop being fools was not an option.

My method worked, and I had their attention. A shaking, unsteady hand waved again, this time prompting them to grab their oars and do as I said. Mimicking a dolphin, I dipped through the waves, being careful not to disappear for too long. A quick flash of the tail would give them enough direction, while keeping me from passing out from airsickness.

After a few hundred yards, I sank closer to the seafloor, away from the impossibly noisy human female who screamed like a crab pinched her with every bump under her vessel, to listen for my clan. Not a single note from one of their songs could be heard, which meant, if Poseidon had any mercy at all, we were far enough away.

But mermaids were crafty. If they suspected I was up to something, they could just be lying in wait. Looking across the murky blue landscape surrounding me revealed no other mermaids, so I swooshed back above the water for one last look around. My eyes had finally adjusted, giving me a better view of the humans I rescued.

The female's long hair tangled in her face, though she made no effort to move it. It was as if she used the veil it provided to hide from her ordeal. The older gentleman to her right held her close, rubbing his white beard against her forehead.

Then there was a boy, not much older than me, watching me with an intense curiosity not at all laced with fright. He leaned over the edge of their plastic lifeboat, trying to close the distance between us as much as he could.

The sun set aglow speckles of green in his otherwise arctic eyes, almost as if they were littered with aquamarine. Dark hair that matched my own clung to his bronze skin, crusted with sea salt and sweat.

He held out his hand, reaching for me. "You're not leaving, are you?"

I gave a slow nod, taken aback by his boldness.

"Please don't." He licked some of the dried mineral from his thick lips, and my heart fluttered in an unfamiliar, unsteady fashion.

Sinking lower, I soaked my gills without dunking my face just long enough to take in a breath. I opened my mouth, prepared to explain that he should continue heading north, away from the danger he couldn't conceive of. That he needed to go, and fast, before it was too late.

But instead of farewell, a song came forth.

SINK

Come swim with me, sailor,
I'll show you the way.
The ocean's your home now,
You'll beg me to stay.

Shocked by the words that came from my own mouth without permission or intent, I slapped my hand over my lips, ignoring the sting.

What in the ocean just happened?

Ms. Star's words sprang into my mind, *Once you have found the human the ocean deems you tied to, your song will come forth without effort.*

No, no, no. This couldn't happen; I wouldn't let it. I would not be responsible for luring this boy to his death. My chest burned, eager to finish the song and perform the hypnosis properly.

Instinct was winning. Before I could act again without control, I dove back under the waves, seeking the safe haven of my grotto. Only feet from the seafloor, a distinctive explosion sounded above me. I cursed to myself, praying I wasn't about to see this human's body on my side of the world. But, when I saw his body fighting the current to swim down toward me, I knew it was too late.

My first verse must have latched on to him, dragging him with me. Heat scorched my throat. As if hypnotized myself by the sight of him, the second verse poured out.

"Come kiss me, sailor,
You'll drink in the sea.
Sink to the seafloor,
Forever with me."

CHAPTER 5

Jewel loitered outside Ms. Star's classroom with a group of other students, preparing for the day's lesson. I murmured some terribly un-mermaid-like obscenities. The plan was to grab her while she was still swimming alone, not hide out behind a big rock trying not to get caught.

Since my big reveal, this was a part of the kingdom I was no longer welcomed in. *Banned* was the term Ms. Star used. While not quite as serious as banished, I still didn't want to get caught trespassing.

"Pssst…" I called in her direction, my voice low but audible. "Jewel."

She glanced over her shoulder, her forehead crinkled in annoyance until she noticed it was me. "Pauline?"

I hushed her, and then motioned for her to come closer.

"What are you doing here?" she asked as she swam toward me. "If Ms. Star finds you here, she'll turn you into crab soup."

"I need your help."

Jewel grinned, shifting her hip out. "What'd you do now? Tell some baby dolphins that humans can snatch them up and eat them for lunch?"

"This is serious. Come to my grotto. I have to show you something."

She waved toward the other merlings. "Uh, class is about to start. Ms. Star is set on 'undoing the damage' you did, so it's kind of mandatory."

"Please, Jewel." I clasped my hands together, offering up my best pleading face. "I would never ask you to ditch if it wasn't life or death."

My best friend sighed, and my heart skipped. I had her. "Life or death, huh? All right. Let's go."

After a round of thank yous, I took her by the wrist and dragged her back to the palace gates, deciding at the last minute to take my secret route around the back. We shimmied through a small crevice in the coral, which let out close to my private grotto.

"Ouch," Jewel complained when a sharp piece of living rock nipped her tail. "Why do we have to go this way? We were just by the gates."

"If we went through the gates, Prawn or one of her drones would harass us. This way, we won't need to explain to anyone why you aren't in class."

"Fine. You owe me, though."

"You have no idea."

When we approached, I moved a heavy boulder from the entrance. Jewel clicked her tongue and said, "Whoa, you're locked up and everything. Must be something *big*."

I opened my mouth, debating whether to tell her before she went inside. Before I could decide, she swooped through the narrow tunnel. Once I secured the rock back in its place, I swam after her, crashing right into her backside when she stopped short.

Turtle grass and bright-colored algae littered the seafloor and walls of my circular safe haven. Wide but private, the rock enclosure opened at the top to let in just enough light to illuminate the only place in the ocean I could call my own. Knickknacks from the human world, given to me by the many men Mother doomed, sat on the natural shelving. They each held a new meaning to me now. No longer was the ship in a bottle Gene gave me a simple toy meant for amusement, but a memory of his time here and a dedication to his unnecessary death.

Though simple and primitive, this grotto was my spot. I slept here and cried here, but, most of all, I let myself truly *be* here.

Jewel's body remained stiff and still. She lifted a tense arm, pointing a finger at the unconscious body asleep on my bed made of rock. A body with legs instead of a tail. "What the squid tentacles is *that*?"

"I don't know what happened." I wrapped my arms around my torso, preparing for the onslaught of reprimands.

"Pauline, I'm pretty sure that's a man. A human man."

"It is."

"Why in the name of Poseidon is there a *human man* in your grotto?"

Panic rose in my chest, kicking out the air and leaving me gasping. "He followed me. Last night after the hunt."

"Oh." Jewel shrugged. "So he's your mate. What's the problem? You look like you're about to hurl."

"He's not my mate, Jewel."

"I bet the queen was thrilled. Two of her daughters to receive a match from the ocean—what an honor. What about Angelique? She must be wicked jealous."

I wrung my fingers together, looking up at her with timid eyes. "They don't exactly know."

"But you said he followed you after the hunt."

After a deep breath in, I spilled the whole story. Her face shifted from one expression to another as I told the tale of rescuing the humans against my mother's order. When I explained how both of us seemed to be in a trance, she flashed an adoring smile as if it was the most romantic thing she had ever heard.

"And then," I continued. "As soon as I kissed him, he passed out cold. I had to drag him down to the grotto myself, and then swim my tailfin back to the clan before they noticed I was missing. Now that he's here, he won't wake up, and I don't know what to do. Jewel, tell me what to do!"

"How in Poseidon's blue ocean am I supposed to know what to do? I've never seduced a sailor before."

"Well, neither have I."

She swayed closer to him, approaching as though he might jump up at any moment. "He is kind of cute though, huh? I've never seen a sailor with such tan skin."

A pang of jealousy pinched at my gut. If he woke up and saw her, so beautiful and brimming with confidence, he wouldn't want me whether the ocean commanded it or not.

I shook my head, banishing the ridiculous thought before it could creep in any farther. If I had my way, he wouldn't be here long enough to want either of us.

"Jewel." I snapped my fingers. "Focus!"

"You're right. Sorry. This is pretty serious."

"Thank you. How long is he supposed to sleep for? Is he just super tired from the transition or something?"

"How am I supposed to know?"

"You're the A student, remember?"

"Yeah, I must've been absent the day Ms. Star told us how to sneak a human male into your grotto, sorry. Have you tried waking him up?"

"I've tried shaking him and yelling at him. Nothing makes him budge."

"Have you tried jabbing a finger in his gills?"

"What? Jewel, that's terrible!"

She shrugged. "Desperate times call for desperate measures. They're probably still sensitive as fresh as they are." Jewel moved a finger in close to his neck. "I could just..."

"No, don't." I jumped between them, a sudden overwhelming need to protect this strange human taking over. "You'll hurt him."

"Aw. That's adorable. You want to make him like your pet or something."

"That's ridiculous. Just imagine how you would feel waking up with strange creatures poking you in your gills."

Jewel scrunched her nose and groaned. "Point taken. So, what are you going to do then?"

"I don't think there's anything else I can do but wait. Maybe he'll wake up on his own."

"All right. *If* he wakes up, you've got to have a plan."

A moment went by in silence as my mind kicked my options back and forth. "I'm going to put him back," I announced with a curt nod.

"You'll kill him. Might as well hand him over to your mother in that case."

"Not if I figure out a way to reverse the transformation."

She let out a loud, condescending snort, and then teased, "C'mon, Pauline. Don't you think if there was a way to do that, your mother would let them go instead of killing them?"

"And risk the humans finding our kingdom? No way! You know how much she despises them. She thinks they're bent on taking over the whole planet, land *and* sea."

"She might be right, you know. I mean, how much do you or I truly know about them?"

"I know the men I have met down here have been good, decent, and kind. They agreed to help us continue our race for nothing in return." I lifted my chin at her, irritation dripping into my voice. "I'll figure something out for him. Even if I have to go meet with Myrtle."

Jewel gasped, covering her gaping mouth with her hand. "You can't be serious. The sea witch is not the answer to this, Pauline. She's wicked. She'll probably eat you if you go near her lair."

"I'll do whatever it takes. Besides, Mother told

me yesterday that she's my aunt. I can't imagine she would gobble up her own niece."

"You better hope you're right." She shook her head and painted on an exasperated grin. "Guess I can't call you kiss-up anymore. Good girls don't usually go around plotting against the queen, let alone their own mother."

I sat on the rock, just next to the sleeping human. My fingers found a lock of his hair, brushing it out of his face to get a better look. "It's my fault he's here. I have to do what's right. No matter the consequences."

"I hope he's worth it, Pauline."

"He is. I can feel it. Something about him... Destiny brought us together to change things."

Jewel rolled her eyes, giving me a look as if to say I'd lost my seashells. "Things have been this way forever. A single mermaid and a human aren't going to change it."

"You're wrong. It hasn't *always* been this way, Jewel. There were mermen once. We didn't have to drag humans to their death to ensure our survival."

She sighed, giving up the fight, and then murmured, "When he does wake up, he's going to freak. Better make sure you're here. He could wander right into Queen Calypso's throne room and get himself aired out."

"That's kind of why I brought you here." I flipped my lashes at her, half-grinning and half-wincing. "There are a few things I need to take care of. Food, for starters. I imagine he'll be hungry. Plus, I promised a peasant I'd deliver some food for her merling.

Besides, I can't hide out here all the time or Mother will get suspicious."

"You want me to human-sit?" Jewel laughed as she rubbed her temples with her fingers. "Pauline, I get that you want to clear your conscience, but—"

"Please, Jewel. I only need your help until he wakes up. After that, I can explain things to him so he won't take off."

"Oh, for Poseidon's sake."

"Please." I stuck out my bottom lip, casting all pride aside to beg. This was bigger than I was.

She stared at me, without saying a word, for a good thirty seconds before finally exhaling an exaggerated huff. "I must be crazy getting involved in this."

Springing off my bed, I leaped into her arms with a squeal, almost toppling her over. "Thank you, thank you, thank you! I promise, I won't take long."

"You better not. I don't want this thing waking up on my watch."

I headed for the opening of the grotto, stopping short at the archway. "Jewel," I said as I turned back around. "Please don't tell anyone. Not even the merlings at school."

"I'm pretty sure that, at this point, if I did say anything, I could be charged as an accessory. Your secret is safe with me."

CHAPTER 6

"I'm surprised you didn't ask one of the servants to make you something."

Fawna hovered in front of the kitchen counter, dicing a tuna filet. In all the sixteen years I'd inhabited this ocean, this was the first time I saw either of my sisters make their own food.

Her mouth twitched until her lips gave way to a half-smile. "The cook never quite gets it right. She always puts in far too much seaweed and never enough tuna."

"I don't even see any seaweed in there." I snatched a piece of fish from her plate and popped it in my mouth. "Since when do you enjoy seafood so much?"

She patted her stomach. "Pregnancy cravings, I guess. This merling will be a carnivore, just watch. I won't get her to touch her Wakame or sea cucumbers to save my life."

"Hm." I glanced at her stomach, wiggling at the thought of having another mermaid growing inside me. The whole thing seemed awfully parasitic and unpleasant.

Opening a cabinet made from wood harvested from sunken ships hundreds of years ago, I pulled out a wicker basket, also taken from the humans.

My chest released a slow, regretting breath as I wondered how many things we owned that were actually ours and not theirs.

Speaking of parasites.

Fawna cleared her throat before blurting out, "I hear you did well at the hunt. Prawn had nothing but good things to say."

"I guess."

"It's a pity you weren't able to find any survivors except the one."

The sound of ripping flesh echoed in my mind, bringing about the man's phantom weight on my skin. I swallowed hard against the bubbling in my stomach. A cold sweat beaded on my forehead for a moment before the ocean whisked it away.

"Are you all right?" Fawna placed a slim hand on my shoulder, her silver eyes watching me in concern.

Pregnancy had stacked years on my sister. For the first time, I realized how much she resembled Mother. She had the same tiny nose and wrinkles around her eyes as the queen. Fawna's white hair would soon turn silver, to match her eyes, the only feature to set the throne's heir apart from its current inhabitant.

"I'm fine," I lied, forcing a small laugh. "I just haven't eaten since yesterday."

"Oh. Join me for lunch, then. There's plenty for two." Her eyes flitted to her stomach. "Well, three."

"Thanks, but I was planning to eat in my grotto."

Fawna nodded, white ringlets catching on a weak current and twirling up. "Sure. Let me help, at least. What are you in the mood for?"

We stuffed the basket full with shrimp, grouper, and sea vegetables. She asked, "Is this all for you? There's enough here to feed an army."

"Uh, yeah. I'm super hungry, what can I say?"

I closed the basket and swam for the exit, not quite reaching it before my oldest sister called to me.

"Oh, Pauline," she said in a twinkling, sticky-sweet voice.

Busted.

I let out a noncommittal hum, but I didn't turn back around.

"Abigail's merling prefers kelp to nori."

A chill of dread cold as ice trickled down my spine. I spun around to confront her, my face numb with fear. But her eyes were soft. No hint of malice could be found in her expression.

"You can breathe, sweetheart," she assured me. "I'm not going to tell anyone."

"Why would you help me?"

Fawna shrugged. "I couldn't in good conscience turn you in for doing the same thing I did just last night."

"*You* brought Abigail food?" I lifted a skeptical brow at her.

"While you all were on the hunt."

"Fawna... I don't know what—"

She closed the space between us, leaning in close with her lips pressed against my ear. "Despite what you think, my dear sister, you are not the only one on their side."

As my legs wobbled, the weight of my body leaned into her. We were swimming in dangerous territory here. My heart wanted to believe she spoke of the humans, but my mind nagged, tossing logic I couldn't fight against into my thoughts. If Princess Fawna took the side of the sailors, she wouldn't have had a hand in drowning Gene.

No. She meant the peasants, no one else.

My cheeks raised in a shaky smile. "We'll have to feed them together sometime, then. I'm certain it would do wonders for the palace's image."

Her lips parted. A whisper started in her throat, but a high-pitched squeak strangled it. Fawna's eyes went wide, the color drained from her face and she clutched at her stomach.

"Fawna." I gasped, holding on as she collapsed into my side. "Are you... are you in labor?"

My sister gritted her teeth and screamed.

"Angelique," I yelled into the next room as I dropped the basket and wrapped my arms around her. "Mother! Someone help."

From across the palace, I heard a *whoosh* as bodies cut through the water. With Fawna clutched against my chest, I thrust my tail to propel us toward the others.

"Princess Pauline!" Prawn breathed heavy. "What's the matter?"

I turned my sister toward her, as if to say *See for yourself.*

My mother's first officer took one look at her, and then snatched her from my hands. "It's time."

"Isn't it too soon?"

"It's earlier than I'd like, but she's far enough along that everything should be all right."

Angelique rushed in, her face flushed from swimming so fast. She took in the scene, and then took Fawna's hand as Prawn guided her to our clinical cavern on the top floor of the palace. Even as accustomed as we were to the darkness on the seafloor, most medical procedures required some light for precision.

I hastened my pace to keep up, but Prawn turned her sharp nose on me. "You should wait here."

"But she's my sister. I want to make sure she's okay."

"She'll be fine, Princess. I'll see to that myself. You're much too young, yet."

"I'm not a merling anymore," I shouted.

Angelique glared at me, her face even redder now. "Then stop acting like one. We need to tend to Fawna now, so stop arguing. We'll send news when we have it."

I fell back, giving them my trademark obedient nod.

If one could swim a hole into the ground, I would have done it. Around and around, in no less than five hundred circles, I patrolled as I waited for word like a good little princess.

Until I heard her scream.

Not a scream of agony and pain that one would expect from birthing. Those kinds of cries filled the palace almost as soon as they got her up the stairs.

This was different. The kind of shriek that came from dread and despair. I stopped pacing at once, watching the ramp leading to the medical cavern for a moment as I tried to talk myself out of meddling.

"Mother, please don't!" Fawna's plea took hold of me like one of the fishermen's hooks, snapping me to the top of the palace as fast as my tailfin could carry me.

Just as my fingers made contact with the knob, the door flew open, slamming against me and sending me flying backward. Mother appeared, holding something wrapped in a red plaid blanket tightly against her chest. She raked her eyes over me, her face unreadable and hard as stone.

I stayed on the floor, cowering on the smooth, wooden plank floor that was moved to the palace from another ransacked ship. The queen returned her gaze forward, stepping over me as if I were plankton, too small to be bothered with.

Only once she disappeared down the corridor did I dare return myself upright. I inched toward the door, peeking my head between the crack to take in the scene.

"Have some puffer fish, Fawna." Angelique handed a bedridden, much smaller version of my oldest sister a plate. "It will calm your nerves."

Instead of taking it, Fawna rolled on her side, facing away from the offering and toward me. Her glossed-over eyes shimmered with tears. They looked right through me, as if I wasn't even there. Grief ran each breath she took ragged.

Desperate to console her, I leaned in. My shoulder brushed against the door, making it creak. Angelique snapped her gaze in my direction, her frown deepening when she noticed it was me.

"What happened?" I asked, moving into the

room. No use hiding now.

Fawna perked up at my voice, forcing herself to pull out of her funk at least a little. "I uh... I had a miscarriage."

Of all of her talents, lying was her greatest gift. This time, though, she faltered. Heartbreak had an unshakable hold on her. Whatever happened, it was terrible.

"Stop treating her like a merling," Angelique snapped. "She wants to be a grown up, let her be one."

"Angelique, please." Fawna raised a hand, silencing her. "This isn't the time."

I pressed my lips into a hard line, turning to our middle sister. As much as I appreciated Fawna's attempt to shield me, Angelique was right; I was not a merling anymore. "Tell me," I insisted. "I can handle it."

"Fawna's merling was a boy."

"That's wonderful. The curse has been lifted. We don't have to rely on the humans anymore."

Angelique snickered. "You are clueless, aren't you? Mother is the one who enacted the curse. Just after conception, every mermaid is brought to the queen to receive a spell, one that will ensure her child, should the ocean gift her one, is born female. For whatever reason, the spell didn't take in this case. It's uncommon, but it does happen."

"That doesn't make any sense. I can't think of a single logical reason Mother would want to prevent mermen from being born."

"That's because you never *knew* a merman. Just

like human males, they're full of the lust for power and greed. They'll do anything to take the throne from us."

Nonsense. Every bit of it was nonsense, and I had been fed enough of it to tell her so. I pointed a finger into her chest. "You never knew a merman either, Angelique. You're not that much older than me. Stop speaking to me as if you hold so much more authority than I do."

"If I were you, Pauline..." Mother's voice boomed over my tirade. "I would stop while you still can. One day, Angelique will be your queen. You'll want to maintain a good standing with her, I'm sure."

I shook my head, refusing to believe what she just said. "Fawna is the oldest. She is next in line for the throne."

"After what I have seen here today, I'm afraid I don't have the confidence in Fawna I once did. Much like you, she's too emotional to see what's best for the clan."

Angelique lifted a conceited nose in the air. I ignored her, instead turning my attention to Fawna. She laid there, staring into space, trying to tune out the world. Her body shook from the effort, a subtle twitch to her cheeks acting as her only betrayal.

"What did you do with my nephew?" I seethed, gritting my teeth.

Queen Calypso laughed, arrogance growing heavier with her breaths in between chuckles. "That beast will be disposed of. Prawn will see to that."

I gasped. "You're going to kill him?"

"Of course not. We aren't cold-blooded humans

going around murdering each other. No, he will be delivered to the sharks. The blood will be in their teeth, not on my hands."

The walls around me closed in from all sides. My chest burned with rage that almost brought me to my knees. My fists clenched at my sides. I needed to leave before my fingers found their way around this witch's throat.

I whipped around to face the bed once more and promised, "I will find your merling, Fawna. No harm will come to him as long as I'm breathing."

CHAPTER
7

"I'm so sorry, Jewel." I flew through the entry-way to my grotto, basket of edibles in hand. As soon as the room came into sight, so did a flying ship in a bottle.

Breaking glass sounded as it collided with the far wall, followed by a feminine shriek.

"Stop, you... you... *human*," Jeweled ordered from underneath my bed.

I peeked around the corner, holding my breath. The boy who was asleep when I left now crouched in a corner, brandishing an oar in my best friend's direction. While his reddened face was hard from a mask of pretend bravery, the squeak in his voice gave him away.

"Stay away from me," he shouted.

"Look." Jewel raised both her hands in the air with palms facing out. "I'm not going to hurt you, okay?"

"Who... or what are you? What am I doing here?"

"If you'll just calm do—"

"Answer me!"

"My name is Jewel. My friend Pauline brought you down here. I'm just waiting with you until she gets back. She'll explain everything, I promise."

"Where is she?"

I sucked in a breath as I swam forward and announced, "I'm right here."

Two sets of eyes turned on me in an instant. Relief washed across Jewel's face as she climbed out from her bunker, while recognition swept over his. I shrank back, surprised when he didn't cower away from me the way he did Jewel.

"You..." The human pointed at me with a shaking finger. "I remember you."

"Good. Then you remember following me."

"Following you?"

"Yes. You jumped in the water after I led your boat to safety."

He squinted at me, cocking his head to the side. "I don't... I only remember you sang to me."

"I didn't mean to. I'm sorry."

"You're sorry for singing?"

"I'm sorry for what my singing did to you."

"What harm could come from singing?"

Jewel placed her hand on my arm and said, "I tried to tell him. He woke up in a panic, thinking he was drowning."

"You said I had gills," he accused.

"You do," she grumbled. "How else do you explain the fact that you're breathing under the water?"

The human moved his arm through the water, mesmerized by the bubbles left in the wake of his motion, as if this was the first time he'd noticed he was under the sea. "What the hell?"

I moved toward him, advancing when he didn't pull away. "What's your name?"

"Edward. Everybody calls me Eddie, though."

"Eddie," I repeated with a warm smile. "A perfectly human name."

"Are you a... mermaid?"

"That's right. You've heard of us?"

He puffed out his chest. "I'm a fisherman. Of course I've heard of you. Plus, there have been tons of books and movies written about you."

"Books and movies? What are those?"

"Moving pictures, paper with words written on them."

"Paper?"

"Uh... human things, I guess. You wouldn't understand."

He was probably right.

"Eddie, when you followed me under the water, I uh... I sort of kissed you." A warm tingle spread across the bridge of my nose. "Like I said, I didn't mean to. When I saw you, I just started singing. Somehow, the song put us both in a trance. You couldn't help jumping in, and I couldn't help... what I did."

He rubbed the back of his neck and cleared his throat. "Okay. So you're telling me I'm a victim of a zombie kiss?"

"What's a zombie?" Jewel asked.

"You know, the undead." He held out his arms and walked with a stiff gait as he groaned. We both stared at him as if he had lost his mind.

"I don't get it," Jewel said.

I added a, "Me neither."

"Tough crowd." He pulled on his collar. "So, you

kissed me. No big deal. There are worse things than a smooch from a pretty mermaid. Still doesn't explain this." He waved his arm, referring to the water.

I reached out to touch him. "May I?"

He watched me, unsure, but nodded after a moment.

My fingers grazed his freshly formed gills. "When I kissed you, you grew these."

His hands flew to the slits now blemishing the side of his neck, clamping my own hand under his on one side. He paled, looking to me for an explanation.

"I have them too, see." I moved my hair to the side to show him. "So does Jewel."

Eddie licked his lips, and then stuttered, "Does... does that mean... Am I one of you?"

"Not quite. You still have your legs and everything."

His knees trembled, so I reached out to help him sit on my bed. "This is insane," he insisted. "It's a dream. A really freaky dream. I'm in a hospital bed, sleeping off the trauma from the shipwreck. Of course I'd dream about mermaids. The ocean almost killed me. It makes perfect sense."

"Eddie..." I held his hand between mine. "You are awake. The ocean *did* take your ship, but you never made it back to dry land."

"That's exactly what you would say in a dream."

Jewel snapped her fingers. "Hey, snap out of it, kid. You're not in a hospital, whatever that is, you're under the ocean. Pauline pretty much saved your life."

"That's not true." I shook my head, denying the commendation.

"Yes, it is. He's the one who jumped in the water after you. He would have drowned if you didn't give him gills."

"He wouldn't have jumped if I could control my mouth."

"It's your power, Pauline. You're not supposed to control it. Manage it, yes, but you'll never control it. You think I can control my telepathy all the time? Poseidon, no. I'm always getting weird interference from mermaids walking by."

"Okay." Eddie stood up, raising his hands to the shape of a T. "Time out. Powers, telepathy, gills. This is too much for me right now."

"He's right," I agreed. "Maybe we should give him some privacy. Let him sort it all out."

"That would be great. Thank you."

Jewel's jaw dropped. "You want to leave the human alone?"

"Eddie needs to think. You would, too, in his situation." I turned to Eddie. "We'll be right outside. You have to promise me you won't leave. Trust me; it wouldn't bode well for you."

He raised his fist, which had only his middle and index fingers extended and spread apart. "Scout's honor."

"I don't know what that means, but I'm going to take it as a promise."

If I had knees, like Eddie, they would have gone unsteady the way his just had when he flashed me a bright, amused smile. The flutter returned to my chest, playing music against my sternum. I waved and backed away, keeping my eyes on him until I swam right into the coral wall behind me.

"Whoops." I giggled, high-pitched and awkward.

"There's a wall there," he pointed out with a wink.

I nodded, perhaps a tad too enthusiastically. *What in Poseidon was wrong with me?* "Yeah. I found that out."

Jewel groaned, and then grabbed my arm. "Ugh. Come on, already."

We swam out into the open ocean, and as soon as the coast was clear, Jewel pinched me.

"Ouch," I squealed.

"What the heck was that?"

I rubbed the red spot her nails left behind. "I was just being friendly."

"You were acting like an idiot."

"I was not!"

She crossed her arms and jutted out her hip.

"All right." I sighed, pressing my hand against my heart to swoon. "I can't help it. He's so cute, isn't he? I don't know. Something about him just makes my tail turn to mush."

"As much as I'd love to enjoy the romance here—you know how I love a good love story—I have to be the good friend and point out that you need to rein it in."

"Come on, Jewel. I was just flirting."

"Look, I'm your best friend. Nobody knows you better than I do, right? You can't get all cutsie with him or you're going to end up attached."

I waved her off. "You're being ridiculous. I'm not

going to get close."

"I don't think so, but maybe I am. Either way, why risk it? You're the one who wants to let him go, remember?"

"Absolutely. It's not going to be a problem. You're right. I need to stop acting like a girl and start acting like a princess. Respectable, calm, and put together."

"Uh..." Jewel pointed over my shoulder. "I hope this doesn't put a damper on the whole 'put together' thing, but there goes your sailor."

I whipped around, screaming, "What?"

Plumes of sand kicked up from the seafloor as the human made a pitiful attempt at a getaway. His heavy legs proved all but useless against the thick salt water he treaded against. His gills expelled bubbles in massive clouds above his head, indicating his breathing to be rapid and uncontrolled.

When I realized he was headed away from the castle and into open water, which was almost devoid of any mermaids at all save a few outcasts and travelers, my shoulders sagged with relief.

"Should I let him wear himself out first or go after him?"

Jewel chuckled, shaking her head. "You better get him before the sharks do. I don't think he can swim at all."

"You better get to class before Ms. Star calls your mother."

"I'll swing by later and see how things are going. Good luck."

Jewel took off toward the square, and I bounded in the other direction. It didn't take me but a few swishes of the tail to catch up to him. Just for kicks, I swam beside him at a snail's pace.

"I thought you promised to stay put," I reprimanded.

Eddie glared up at me through black eyebrows, his blue eyes almost glowing. "Let me go."

"You don't have any idea what's out there, Eddie. You're much safer in the grotto."

"There's no way I'm going to let you keep me penned up like a dog."

"What's a dog?"

He turned on me, stopping me in an instant. Anger blazed through his pupils, almost burning me as their gaze fell on my skin. "You turned me into a monster."

"Oh. Is that what I am to you? A monster?" I caught my bottom lip between my teeth, forbidding it to quiver.

The creases around his eyes softened a little. I thought he might apologize. At least, I hoped he would, but some poisonous thought penetrated his mind and he tensed up again.

"Forget it," he said as he resumed his trudging.

"Listen, I'm sorry, okay? I swear I didn't have any control over what I did, not that I would've made a different decision if I had a clear head. If I hadn't kissed you, you would have drowned."

"That should have been my choice to make."

"Eddie, you would have *died*." Tears stung in the corners of my eyes, but I blinked them back. "I couldn't watch you suffer like that." *The way I had to watch Gene.*

SINK

"So you turned me into a merman instead?"

"You're not a merman. Not even close." I flicked my tail at him. "No scales. Just gills."

The start of a smile twisted on his lips. "No big deal then, huh?" The spark of amusement faded just as fast as it appeared. "I can't ever go home, can I?"

My gut ached as if it were wrapped in one of the human's fishing lines and squeezed. I shook my head, slow and solemn. "No, you can't. I'm sorry, Eddie."

He took in a breath, glanced around, and then looked back at me. "Don't sweat it. I guess living with the fish won't be so bad. Maybe I'll even learn how to catch a few. Of course, my dad won't be around to see it, but hey. You win some, you lose some."

Though his words were soothing, my heart still felt the pain he tried to conceal. Because of me, he would never see his family again. Regret gnawed at my insides. As kind as he was to attempt to save my feelings, I couldn't accept the break. In the end, I would chew myself up before he would even take a bite.

Eddie lifted a heavy leg, taking another step away from the grotto just as the sound of a merling playing in the distance came into earshot.

I sucked in a sharp inhale. "Where are you going?"

"Just want to check this place out. See what my new digs are like."

"We have to go back." The girl's shrill voice came closer. I lunged for Eddie, but he wiggled away. "Eddie, please. We have to return to the grotto."

"I will. I just want to take a look around."

"It's dangerous out there."

"Don't worry your pretty little mermaid head. I'll keep an eye out for sharks. Swam with them once. I was in a cage then, but this doesn't scare me, either."

Tail swishes. Two of them, and dangerously close.

"Believe me, sharks are the least of your worries."

"What could possibly be worse than sharks?" He took another step.

A duo of fuzzy figures near the palace came into view, and I panicked. Before I could stop myself, I flung my body on top of Eddie's, tackling him to the seafloor. He grunted, but he held his breath when my hair enveloped us, wrapping us in our own little cocoon. Nose to nose, my gills took in his exhalations, sending a shudder through my limbs.

His hands cupped my shoulders, but he didn't push me away. "What are you so afraid of, Pauline?"

"They're going to kill you," I whispered, regretting the warning as soon as it left my lips.

CHAPTER 8

"You have some explaining to do, Pauline."

Eddie sat across from me on the floor of my grotto, his legs contorted in the shape of a pretzel. I shivered at the sight, wondering how in the ocean he could twist in such a way without injuring himself.

Before sitting down to pick at the food I brought, we cleaned up the broken glass and returned my room to the less-chaotic state it was in before his episode. I couldn't deny using the cleaning as a way of putting off the inevitable. Now that we were through, it was time to explain what we were up against.

"You're not going to like what I have to tell you," I advised as I popped a piece of seaweed in my mouth.

"That's too bad, because I've loved everything you've had to say so far."

"Sarcasm from the human." I waggled my eyebrows at him. "How unexpected."

He laughed, and the masculine sound tightened my chest, robbing me of air. "You say that like you've known a few of us."

"I've had the pleasure a time or two."

"Wow. I feel way less special now. Just how many humans *have* you kissed?"

Heat burned my face, and I was sure my cheeks were as red as a snapper. "It wasn't me who brought them down here. You were my first, which is why I seem as though I have no idea what I'm doing. I don't."

"So, there are other mermaids who can do what you do?"

I nodded. "They're much less kind about it, I assure you."

"How do you mean?"

My tail shifted from under me, and I joined him on the seafloor. "There aren't any mermen left in the ocean," I said bluntly. "Growing up, I was told this was the result of a curse that went back hundreds of years. Now, I'm not so sure. I believe the queen killed them off to ensure the throne would remain hers, not fall into the hands of a merman who wished to take it from her. The details, well, I don't know those yet. I'm working on it."

"Okay." He closed one eye, as if hiding from his next question. "So, how do you... make more mermaids without the mermen?"

"That's where the humans come in. We never sink a ship on purpose, but when we hear one coming down, we sing to the survivors. If one is entranced by our song, the way you were, he is brought down to um... make a merling."

Now Eddie was the one blushing. His cheeks stained pink, and he cleared his throat. "Look, I'm only seventeen. I don't think I'm ready to start making merlings just yet."

"I'm not finished." I stifled a giggle at his reaction and continued. "I only just found out this part a few days ago, but after the human has served his purpose, Queen Calypso puts him to death."

And just like that, the blush faded until his face was almost as white as mine. "She does what, now?"

"Don't worry," I hurried. "I'm not going to let that happen to you. That's why it's so important you stay in here, so Mother doesn't find out you're here."

"Mother?" he echoed.

"Yes. The queen is my mother, as much as I hate to claim it."

"You're a princess, then."

"That's right."

Eddie scratched his head. "But you live in a grotto. I saw the palace not far in the distance. If you're a princess, why aren't you there?"

"I like my space." I shrugged, and then waved around the room at the human artifacts I collected. "Plus, Mother wouldn't let me keep these things in the palace. She said they stink of human. They're all I have to remember all the men she executed. I like having them around."

"You like us even though you were taught to hate us. That's strange."

"I guess," I admitted. "Maybe I would believe her if she wasn't the one going about murdering people. She's the one who appears to be the villain right now, not you."

"I like you, Pauline." He brushed a long, black wave of my hair over my shoulder, and I shivered. "You have a good head on your shoulders. Maybe you should be the one on the throne instead of her."

"Thank you, but I have no desire to take her seat."

He took a slice of nori, filling it with a thin fillet of grouper. After rolling them together, he pulled a knife out of his pocket, slicing the roll into inch-wide chunks. I watched as he took a bite and groaned, as if it was the most delicious thing he had ever tasted. When he licked a stray speck of green from his lips, I realized how much I wished I could remember what our kiss was like.

"Strange way to eat," I commented.

"Sushi," he said through a mouth full of food. "One of my sister's favorites. I never liked it much, but I'm so hungry I could eat anything. It's much better when it's this fresh, though. She'd die right about now. Do you have any sisters?"

I nodded. "I have two. One just had a merling, actually."

"That's nice. Too bad the poor guy she had it with is dead, though."

A sudden itch to move the conversation away from my nephew nipped at me. I couldn't bear the thought of him alone out in the ocean, waiting for the sharks to come and gobble him up like bait. "I don't remember seeing a girl in your lifeboat, only a woman."

"No, she hates fishing. She stayed home with my mom. I went with my grandparents and my father."

"The older gentleman in the raft with you—that was your grandfather?"

He stopped chewing, and his jaw flexed. "Yeah. We were looking for my dad when you came. I hope he's all right."

I opened my mouth, prepared to tell him I found his father's body, lifeless and sinking, but I decided against it. By now, the sharks had him. There was no reason to take away his last bit of hope. He should cling to it for dear life.

"So, is this Atlantis?" he asked, swallowing his food.

"Of course not. Atlantis is almost half an ocean away. This is Atargatis."

"You've been to Atlantis?"

"Oh, no. It's the sunken city of the humans, filled with their evil and reeking with their scent—so my mother says."

"Hm. Makes me wonder what she's hiding there."

"What do you mean?"

"If she's tried so hard to convince you to stay away, she must have something there she doesn't want you to find."

I could have fallen back when his words barreled into me. The thought had never crossed my mind that she might be hiding something there, but it made perfect sense.

"Wait a minute." I arched a brow at him. "How do you know of Atlantis?"

"Ah, humans have been talking about it forever. People have spent their fortunes trying to find it. We know it's out there, just can't figure out where to look. Man, I'd love to go there. I'd be the first person to step foot in Atlantis in like, a thousand years."

"So, we'll go there."

"Yeah?"

"One day. I have to find out how to get there.

Maybe I can locate a map or something."

"You aren't worried about what your mom will say?"

"I'm already guilty of harboring a human. There isn't a much greater crime than that."

"Sorry to be the one to turn you into a felon."

"A felon?" I scrunched my nose at him. "You speak so strange."

"You're the one who talks funny. You're so proper, annunciating every syllable like you're reading a poem."

"Habit of my royal training, I guess. I can try to be crasser, if it will make you more comfortable."

He shook his head, placing his hand on my shoulder. "Don't change it. You sound beautiful." His fingers traced the raised skin on my bicep before he moved closer to examine the scar. "Where'd you get this?"

"I got too curious when I was a merling. Swam too close to the surface. A fisherman latched on to me. I was so small, maybe five or six years old. It only took him a few minutes to drag me up to the surface."

Eddie's mouth fell open, and he asked, "He saw you?"

"I don't see how he couldn't have. This purple tail is a dead giveaway. I never actually broke through the water. My oldest sister Fawna got me off the hook just a second before, but I was close enough and the water is so clear here. He had to have seen me."

"That must've hurt."

"You have no idea. The only way to get it out so quickly was to rip it."

He closed a protective hand over the pink link, hissing through his teeth. "Ouch. I can't believe your mother let you get so close to a fishing boat."

"She wasn't with us. It was just Fawna and me. No way Mother would've allowed us anywhere near a ship. Well, not one topside anyway."

"But your sister, she wasn't worried about what could happen? I mean, I'm not saying your mother is right and all humans are evil, but if they caught you... Let's just say you'd probably be on the bad end of a science study."

"When I was younger, Fawna always liked to bring me with her to study the humans. I guess our curiosity drowned out the risk at the time."

"I'd like to meet her one day. Doesn't sound like she's one itching to watch the humans killed."

I thought about that for a moment, quiet and still. Remembering the adventures she took me on when I was younger made me recall a different side to Fawna I had long forgotten. We followed ships together, imagining out loud what it must be like to live on land. She would tell me about the humans she watched from a distance, all their little quirks and habits she found both odd and fascinating. Fawna became so good at lying to cover up our whereabouts, but it wasn't a talent I shared.

Once when Mother asked me where we spent the afternoon, I tried to cover it up. I wove a tale about salvaging a shipwreck. It all sounded well and good, and plausible to boot, until she asked *where* this mystery ship was so she could send out additional scouts. That was when I broke down and told her the truth.

It became clear to Fawna that she couldn't include me on her explorations, not if she wanted them kept secret. I was the obedient daughter, always doing what the queen commanded and unable to rebel. She pulled away from me, suddenly and all at once, breaking my heart in the process. Her obsession with the humans and their ways was our downfall.

Thinking back on the years, I could not recall a single instance where Fawna spoke against the humans. Not once did she ever mention their wicked ways or their lust for world domination.

But she did watch Gene die without lifting a finger to stop it. For that, I could never forgive her. Whether she believed them to be beasts or not was irrelevant; by her inaction, she chose her side.

"Pauline." Eddie watched me, studying my face as if he was trying to read my mind. "Are you all right?"

I nodded, blinking back the memory. "Of course. I don't think meeting Fawna is a great idea, that's all."

"Whatever you think is best. You know your sister and this situation better than I do."

"Yes," I replied, unsure of the accuracy of his claim. I still had no idea what the best course of action was. All I could do was act according to instinct. Sixteen short years of instinct.

"So, I can't help but wonder. What's the plan here? Am I just supposed to spend the rest of my life locked in your bedroom? Because I have to tell you, I don't do well in small spaces for long."

"I don't exactly have a plan, per se. I'm working on it, though."

Eddie jumped to his feet, a playful bounce in his step. "You'll come up with something. I have faith in you."

"You barely know me."

"You're risking an awful lot to keep me safe. That tells me all I need to know."

A funny feeling let loose in my torso, as if I swallowed a jellyfish whole and its tentacles had wrapped around my insides. No one had ever trusted me in such a way. Here was this human, in a strange world, putting his faith and life in the hands of a being alien to him.

"Pauline." Angelique's muffled call penetrated the boulder that kept us safe from the outside world.

My body froze in place. I gaped at the entrance, trying to figure out my next move. If I didn't answer, perhaps she would think I wasn't here and go away. Then again, there was always the chance she would invite herself in and check for herself.

The risk was too great. I turned to Eddie. "You have to hide."

He looked around the room and threw up his hands. "Hide where? You don't exactly have a closet I can duck into."

"What's a—never mind. Just stay quiet."

"Maybe it's just blue coming back to check in."

"Who?"

"You know, your friend with the blue hair. She

said she was coming back."

"Her name is Jewel and, I promise you, that's not her. It's my sister, Angelique. She's just as treacherous as my mother. Trust me."

"All right, all right. But if I hear a struggle, I'm coming out swinging."

An image of Eddie, flailing his human appendages around while my sister swatted him with her tail, flashed, and a heavy, loud belly laugh surfaced. "There isn't going to be a fight, Eddie. But thanks for the backup."

"Pauline," Angelique shouted again. "Are you in there?"

"Stay put," I whispered to Eddie before swimming through the corridor. I pushed the giant rock aside, darted out, and then returned it to block the entrance.

CHAPTER 9

Angelique motioned toward the barricade. "What's with the rock?"

Attempting to channel some of Fawna's strength of deception, I offered a nonchalant shrug. I leaned my back against the boulder and said, "I just thought now that I'm not a merling, I might be entitled to a bit of privacy."

"You might get more privacy if you moved back in the palace. There's no telling what kind of riffraff might come along and make themselves at home here. Not that there's anything worth taking." She shuddered. "Human things."

I bit my tongue, trying my best to ignore the insult against Eddie. "Everyone in the kingdom knows this is my grotto. I'm not concerned. What can I do for you, Angelique?"

"Mother wishes to see you."

"You've become her messenger, I see. This is the second time in two days you've collected me on her behalf. Prawn will be jealous."

My sister narrowed her eyes on me, pursing her lips. "I do as my queen asks me to do."

"Of course you do. May I ask the reason for today's visit? Am I being charged with another crime?

I'd like to be prepared if another sentencing is at hand."

"This is a more informal meeting. No sentencing and no peasants this time. It will be Fawna, you, and me in attendance, no one else."

"Do you think right now is the best time? I don't know that Fawna is in well enough condition to tackle family affairs."

"Our sister is healing just fine, I assure you. She carries the royal bloodline, and, as such, she is expected to, pardon the human expression, suck it up."

I let out a noise somewhere between a laugh and a tsk, well aware of how condescending it came off. "How empathetic of you."

"For Poseidon's sake, Pauline. I haven't the patience to quarrel with you about this. This is a matter of life and death."

"Whose life?" I asked to be difficult.

Angelique's lips pulled back, exposing her sharp, white teeth in a hideous, malevolent grin. "Why, yours, little one."

I straightened my spine. Every ounce of my new-found spunk drained from my body. Suddenly, I was my old compliant, agreeable self again. All it took was a reminder as to what consequence I might face.

"I see I have your attention," she remarked, a satisfied complacency setting her aglow.

Without my permission, my chin moved up and down with a nod.

"Good. Let's go." She swam toward the palace as I debated warning Eddie.

Was it possible Queen Calypso knew about him

somehow?

Maybe Angelique was luring me away so the guards could swarm my grotto and abduct him. They would air him out to dry, no doubt making me watch just before they dragged me up to the surface beside him to share in his fate.

Chills took hold of me. Goose bumps formed on my skin. I kept a flat hand on the boulder, terrified of what would happen the second I let it go.

"You're going to upset Mother further," Angelique warned over her shoulder, but she kept swimming.

She was right. The longer I made the queen wait, the harsher her treatment would be. Besides, if I thought about it, I knew deep inside if she was aware of Eddie, Mother would be out here herself. The embarrassment would be too much to allow anyone else to witness her daughter bringing home a stinking human.

I took in a steady breath and removed my shaking hand from the rock with a shove. As I floated away from my sanctuary, I was relieved at what I heard.

Nothing. No rushing guards, no attack on Eddie. Just quiet. The silence comforted me, giving me enough confidence to swim out in the open water without hesitation. Whatever awaited me in the palace had nothing to do with my Eddie, which meant I could bear it just fine.

Angelique led me through the throne room. The gigantic room was empty, an unusual sight to say the least. The swish of our tails sounded loud in the open space; each bubble that popped in our wake might as well have been one of the human's bombs detonating. A sound I'd heard only once, but it would stay engrained in my memory forever.

An eerie air filled the place, and I shivered.

"Where is everyone?" I asked.

"Mother had the palace evacuated for the evening. The servants get some time off, and we have the privacy we need."

"The palace is creepy vacant. I don't like it."

She laughed as she set her hand on a statute of Poseidon beside Mother's throne. "If you think a bare room is spooky, you're definitely not going to like this."

The white marble statue beside her was almost as tall as she was if her tail started at the floor. But since she floated a foot off the ground, she towered over it. Her palm closed over the top of the bearded man's bald spot, and then pressed downward.

Poseidon's head collapsed into his shoulders, disappearing beneath his chiseled collarbone. A creak rattled the room, and Mother's throne lifted from the seafloor, then tilted back, exposing a hidden hole under its shining gold frame.

An artificial light shone from within, reflecting green off Angelique's brown eyes. "After you," she offered with a sarcastic half bow.

I sank into the opening, slow and trembling. All the years I lived in the palace, a dungeon sat below my tail, and I never even knew it. Knowing my mother, there was no telling what secrets she kept hidden there.

SINK

The water around me chilled as the darkness drank me in, swallowing me whole. The sickly green light lured me closer like a fish drawn to a dancing bug on the surface of the ocean. As I descended deeper into the underwater cavern, a cauldron came into view. A fern-colored liquid bubbled from inside, expelling a neon gas that illuminated the room. Behind it, two mermaid silhouettes flickered.

A foreboding tingle jolted through my body, stopping my descent. Angelique shoved from behind, inching me forward. "Don't be such a baby."

"It's all right, Pauline." Fawna's feminine voice echoed from somewhere in the blackness. "There's nothing to fear."

I sucked in a breath from my nose, releasing a steady stream of bubbles from my mouth as I let it go. Finally, figures recognizable as my eldest sister and my mother came into focus.

Within a few moments, my eyes adjusted to this new level of obscurity, enabling me to make out my surroundings. A massive oak bureau sat beside the cauldron, with various maps and correspondence held in place with shards of metal, no doubt scavenged along with the desk. Though badly worn and decaying from the constant exposure, most of the writing was still legible.

"What's all this?" I wondered aloud, swimming closer to get a better look.

Mother tapped her nails on a stack of papers. "This is none of your concern."

I pointed toward the boiling potion between us. "And the witchcraft? Not my business, either, I suspect."

Mother leaned forward and sniffed the concoction, her eyes rolling in the back of her head. "Quite the contrary. You'll find understanding from this."

"Sorcery is forbidden."

"For the common folk, yes. The queen, as you know, abides by a different set of rules."

Evil clawed at my instincts, issuing a silent command to get as far away from this place as possible. It took every ounce of control I had not to allow my tail to take off swimming back where I came from. There was a safety to be had in familiarity, and this dungeon was nothing I wanted to know.

I took a stab at an excuse. "And since Fawna and I aren't in line for the throne, perhaps this is a lesson Angelique could attend on her own."

"You will stay." Mother's tone oozed impatience, but it was her eyes that put an end to my protest. Black beads void of anything but hatred. "Come closer."

As ordered, I swished forward until the magical fumes choked me. My lungs filled with a corrosive burn, causing me to hack a flemy cough into my fist. "Good Poseidon, what's in that?"

The queen moved her hand over the smoke, which instantly dissolved at her touch. "I believe, considering recent events and lapses in judgement, it is time you girls learned the truth about everything."

Fawna stayed in the shadows, but Angelique bounded forward, eager to hear every word Mother had to say. Though I loitered in place for a moment,

I couldn't keep my curiosity at bay.

She called Fawna to join us, and I couldn't help but notice my sister's face was still ashen from her ordeal. My chest ached for the emptiness that no doubt consumed her. The loss she suffered at the hands of her own mother would be enough to turn even the brightest mermaid cold. I prayed to Poseidon she managed to cling to her warmth with all her strength.

My fingers found hers, and I squeezed, a silent way of offering comfort. To my surprise, she blinked at me, and then gripped my hand tight, as if letting it go meant losing her grip on herself.

Mother's hands, wrinkled and aged far beyond the skin on her face, gripped a vial full of a purple substance corked at the top. She removed the blockage, and then tossed the whole container in the cauldron to prevent the contents from catching on the water instead of making it to its intended destination.

The addition hit the putrid green with an explosion of light and sound. We three sisters shielded our eyes, but Mother was unfazed. Caustic smog climbed up again from the pot in tendrils that curled around us, both as a group and individually.

"A story will unfold within," Mother said, her voice deeper and crackled. "You'll watch it until its end."

As promised, the wisps of smoke shrank back into the mixture, transforming into images and shadows that were distorted at first, but when they focused, two mermaids showed as crystal clear reflections.

No. One mermaid and one merman, hiding in a grotto and clutching one other for dear life.

An odd sense of knowing fixed itself on me. The mermaid in the cauldron, with silver hair and a bejeweled grown even grander than the one Mother wore, was someone I knew. And if my gut could be believed, I knew her intimately.

She turned her face, revealing her features to me, and I gasped. The similarities to Fawna were uncanny. This young girl wore the same small nose, same long hair. It was her eyes, however, that set her apart. Instead of Fawna's silver irises, this mermaid's eyes shined the same chocolate shade as Angelique's.

I knew her, though I couldn't place how. I shouldn't, but I did. Judging by the style of the seashells covering her breasts, the teenager the magic showed us was from at least a hundred years ago.

It was Angelique who said what I was thinking.

"Mother." Her eyes shot across the cauldron, accusation written across her face. "This is you. I mean, your eyes are different now, but I just know it is."

Queen Calypso conceded with a gentle nod. "Close your eyes. All of you."

Though confused, I wouldn't argue the request. My eyelids shut almost on instinct, as I was sure my sisters' did as well. An internal shock rattled my bones and my joints convulsed, tensing my limbs straight as sticks. A warmth spread across my body as magic seeped in, followed by a piercing screech penetrating my eardrums.

Instinct called me to cover my ears and protect

myself from the noise, but that wasn't going to happen. Whatever dark enchantment Mother cast on us, it held my will captive, preventing so much as a whimper from escaping.

The deafening noise faded, replaced by the familiar sound of ocean crashing against the shoreline. Slowly, my functions returned to my command. As soon as I was able, I burst my eyelids open, gasping for air as if the inability to see choked the life out of me. Calm returned to me for a short moment until voices came from within my mind.

"Do you love me?" a woman asked, her voice a more innocent, less deviant one than my mother's, but still recognizable as hers.

I glanced at my sisters. Fawna fidgeted with her hands, her eyes wide with fear. Angelique floated on the tip of her tail, hopping in place, close to bursting with excitement. The cauldron called to me, so I returned my attention to it.

The mermaid gazed at the merman with a sort of desperate longing. Her eyes begged him for the answer she needed to hear, and her caller did not disappoint.

"Of course I love you, Calypso."

"Good. Then let's swim far away from here. We can be together then."

"I can't allow you to leave your kingdom, Princess. Your people need you. Your mother loves you, too."

"If my mother loved me, she would never ask me to choose. Your lack of royal blood should have no say on our right to be together."

"Her duty is to her kingdom, and so is yours."

"But I choose you, Dante."

The merman shook his head. His face remained stone cold and aloof, while Mother wept at his tail. "All we can have is tonight, Calypso. Nothing more."

A younger version of my mother wiped her face clean and sniffed. "Then I will cherish the night with all my heart."

She leaned in, parting her lips for a kiss. Dante lifted his hand, brought it to her shoulder, and squeezed.

At first, the gesture seemed affectionate, sweet even, but when the mermaid's face twisted in pain, I noticed the placement. His thumb pressed down on the muscle behind her collarbone, a pressure point Ms. Star taught us to use on the humans in case one turned violent. Mother's mouth fell open when she made a pitiful attempt at a scream. Before she could manage, her eyes closed and her body went limp.

The sorry excuse of a merman didn't even bother to lay the princess down gently before he ripped the diamond-and-gemstone beset tiara from her hair. Her body hit the seafloor hard, the back of her head making impact with a sharp piece of coral. Blood spiraled up, spiraling into the current as if it belonged in the sea.

I wanted to reach out, to shake the mirage and wake her up. She shouldn't sleep with a concussion. My heart yearned to comfort her, to be there for this strange innocent who was once upon a time my mother. It was what happened to her body next, however, that shook me from my grief.

The young mermaid's tail lost some of its sheen, now looking like one belonging to an elder. Her silver hair greyed a bit, and deep wrinkles set on her face. Liver spots formed all over her limbs and torso. In front of my eyes, this teenage merling aged at least sixty years.

Mother, my mother of today, shouted, "Cease," and the sounds and hallucinations stopped.

"I don't understand," I stammered. "What happened to you?"

"You mean—why did I turn into a hideous beast?" she screamed, mad with fury dredged up from her own reflected memory.

"Mother," Fawna interjected. "That isn't what she meant. But you... changed when he took your crown."

Angelique bobbed her head up and down with furious speed. "You aged."

"That's right," Mother said. "I grew *old*. Because, my dearest daughters, I *am* old. Three hundred years, give or take. I stopped counting."

I gripped the desk behind me for support. The room spun around me. Panic set in my chest. While it took some concentration, I breathed through the burn. Fawna rubbed my back with a gentle hand, but Angelique kept the questions coming, as if there was nothing at all startling with Mother's revelation.

"But you don't look like that anymore. You're beautiful again!"

"That crown provided the one most coveted gift in the ocean. Immortality. As long as I wore it on my head, I would never age. When he removed it, my body returned to its natural state of age."

"You must've hunted him down, right? Stolen your crown back and made him pay. With his life, no doubt."

Angelique's enthusiasm only exacerbated my queasiness. She spoke as if this was story time, a fun fairy tale concocted from some mad writer's imagination. But this wasn't. This was our lives and the implications were incredible.

Queen Calypso's lips fell into a deep frown. "He did pay, along with every merman in the ocean, plus a few mermaids who got in my way. The crown, however, was lost to me. A family heirloom, one of only two to ever exist, gone forever."

"Who had the other?" I asked, the brick in my stomach growing heavier every second.

"Your grandmother." Her voice remained steady.

"You took it from her, didn't you?"

Mother crossed her arms in front of herself, perhaps preparing for the barrage of judgement to come. "She couldn't be reasoned with, you see. It was her fault I was in such a predicament in the first place."

"Mother," I gasped. "You didn't kill her, did you? Please tell me you didn't murder your own mother. Even you aren't that heartless."

"Of course I killed her, simple girl. I gave her the option to give me the crown and she refused, so I took it by force."

A gag choked me. My gills flapped rapidly, pulling air in as fast as they could. Woozy cloudiness fell over my eyes. Killing her own flesh and blood—how could she sleep at night?

Angelique brushed the gold resting on top of Mother's head with a careful finger. "So the crown you wear now, it's grandmother's?"

"No. The crown your grandmother wore was bestowed with magic meant only for her. It did nothing for me."

"Grandmother died for nothing," Fawna pointed out with a soft acceptance to her voice. Though we never knew her, the missing member of our family dying for nothing was a hard blow to all of us, or at the very least, Fawna and me. Angelique remained enamored with the tale.

"Where is it, then?" I looked around the room, expecting to find it hidden amongst the treasures.

The queen continued. "It seems my mother assigned an heir for whom the magic was reassigned. My sister, Myrtle."

"That's why you banished her," Angelique speculated, but Mother shook her head.

"Once Myrtle saw my condition, we sought out every sorcerer we knew about. She promised we would find a way to fashion another tiara. We never did find a witch to help, but we did find this." She banged her knuckle down on top of a stack of books. "An ancient book containing the dark magic of the entire ocean."

My scalp prickled as I said, "You created another one with *dark magic*."

"Without the help of my sister. Myrtle claimed the price was too steep. The spell required a mixture of blood belonging to a merman and a human male. She touted about goodness and not sacrificing others for the sake of ourselves. Selflessness... a childish notion."

"You killed them yourself, then," Fawna said. "A merman and a human."

"I didn't just kill one of each," Mother bragged. "The way I reasoned, the more blood, the more powerful the magic. With Mother gone and me the eldest, I took the throne. My first order was to have every single merman in the ocean beheaded. Dante's execution I handled myself."

My hands flew to my neck, covering the tender flesh in a sudden flash of protectiveness.

A sadistic smile took its place on her face. "I'll admit that I may have gotten carried away. Especially if you consider my magic wasn't anywhere close to strong enough on my own to make the spell last for more than a decade or so. Now, with no more mermen, I have to rely on human blood to carry the invocation. As diluted and polluted as their blood is, it only lasts five years at best.

"Don't look at me that way," Mother demanded. "As if you have a right to such condescension. You have no idea what I've went through."

"Mother..." Fawna stepped between us. "Perhaps she isn't of an age yet to understand. Heartbreak... it's a learned pain, understandable only through experience."

"And you believe yourself to be more knowledgeable of such things, Fawna?"

"I just lost my child." My oldest sister blinked, fighting hard against the tears that shined in her eyes. "There is no greater heartache that I can think of."

"Consider yourself lucky, then. There are far greater tragedies to be had in this life."

"What happened to Myrtle?" I asked over Fawna's shoulder. "Did you banish her because she wouldn't go along with your plan?"

Queen Calypso leaned in, shaking her head. "That sea witch tried to stop me. She conjured up spell after spell, trying to throw me off course. Myrtle even harbored mermen, hiding them from me. One day, I had enough. I sent her away. Far enough away that her magic could never touch me and she could never interfere again."

"She could just sneak back into Atargatis," Angelique pointed out. "Perhaps attack when you're sleeping and not expecting it. Even Prawn has to rest; she can't stand guard day and night."

"Which is why I cast my own little spell. A magical barrier surrounds our kingdom. If Myrtle so much as passes a finger through it, she disintegrates. She is stuck in her isolation. Alone and suffering."

Fawna shifted in front of me. Tension swelled in her back as Mother tapped unconsciously at the map on the desk beside her. I glanced at it, recognizing some of the markings.

An elongated strip of land from the north called *Florida* and to our south, *Puerto Rico*. Atargatis sat just to the east of a place called Cuba, in the center of an area a sailor had marked off with a giant triangle. *The Bermuda Triangle* was scrawled above it. Just under Mother's index finger was a red smudge, the mark made from underwater ink to keep it from fading like the human's.

I found her.

CHAPTER 10

"You want me to do what now?" Jewel sat in front of a mirror brushing her long, blue hair, her eyes fixed on my reflection. Now that it wasn't pulled back, it flowed to the small of her back, thick and beautiful.

"I need you to create a diversion."

"Okay." She drew out the word, as if my request was the most outrageous one she could think of. "Who would I be distracting exactly?"

"Prawn. Oh, and my mother."

She waved her hands in front of herself, slicing her flat palms through the water and shaking her head. "Uh-uh. No way am I getting myself arrested for your human pet. I'm in deep enough as it is. Sorry, but I'm too pretty to get locked up. You do it."

"Yes, you're gorgeous." I rolled my eyes, but smiled. "You're also the best actress I know. There's no way I can keep myself together well enough to pull it off. I've got to get to Myrtle, and the only way I can find her is if I get that map."

Jewel thought for a moment, and then said, "Do you really think I'm a great actress?"

"The best."

"I just... I don't even know how I would *do* that,

Pauline. Prawn is pretty much a living statue outside that gate. Your mom, she doesn't get off that throne for anything but dinner."

"Fake an injury or something. Say you broke your tail."

"You want me to swim up to Prawn and tell her I broke my tail? Yeah, she won't buy that. She'll kind of notice the whole swimming part, and the jig will be up."

"You're right. Think, think, think. It has to be something urgent. Something that will get their attention and keep it long enough for me to get in and out."

"Something to do with humans ought to do it. Oh, I know. I could tell them I found a human hiding in a grotto."

I took her by the shoulders and whipped her around, brining my face just an inch away from hers. "Don't even joke about that. You promised."

"Holy Poseidon." She shoved me away, and I let her. "I wasn't serious, you know. A promise is a promise."

"Sorry. It's just, I feel like I owe it to Eddie to give this my best shot."

Jewel crossed her arms in front of her chest. "Once you have the map... what then? Are you really going to take off to the middle of the ocean and knock on your auntie's door? Like, 'Hey, I know we've never met, but I'm your long-lost niece. The daughter of the evil chick who banished you. Oh, and by the way, I brought a human.'"

"I don't see a better option."

"Look, Pauline. She's not going to invite you in for nori and salmon."

"That's not what I'm expecting at all."

"Then what *are* you expecting?"

"I don't know," I admitted with a shrug. "Maybe that she'll understand where I'm coming from. The way Mother told it, Myrtle is pretty sympathetic to humans. She didn't like the way my mother does things, and neither do I. I guess I'm hoping I'll finally find someone who doesn't look at humans like a sub-species only good for keeping a queen alive past her expiration date."

Jewel pressed her lips together, and then offered one sharp nod. "Okay. I get it. I haven't bonded with the humans like you have, so I can't relate to what you're going through. But you're my best friend. I guess I have to help you."

"No, Jewel. You don't have to do anything. I'm asking you to; that doesn't make you obligated."

"Sure it does, and that's all right. You'd do the same for me. If we're going to do this, though, we're going to do it right."

I lifted a brow and grinned like a sea ray. "Have you any bright ideas, my resident trouble-making expert?"

"You know I do. Here's how it's going to go down. First, you've got to go in the palace with your mother. If she sees us together, it's automatically going to look suspicious."

"We're together all the time. I don't see why she'd find that odd."

"Just let me finish. I'm going to swim up to Prawn,

tell her I was playing with some dolphins near the surface and I found a life raft with a few humans in it. *Live* humans. If you're with me, they won't buy it. By now, I think they know you're not about to point them in the direction of any helpless sailors or fishermen."

"That'll get Prawn moving. What about Mom?"

"That's where you come in. You need to set the scene. Make a snide comment about how the last hunt was a disaster and maybe Prawn isn't as capable as she thinks. If the queen is as desperate for human blood as you say she is, she'll want to tag along to make sure the job gets done right."

"Jewel, you're a genius." I hugged her tightly.

If I had toes, I would've been tripping on them as I approached the castle gate. Prawn, wearing an awfully sour scowl, spared me but a flick of her eyes before returning them forward again.

"Good morning, Prawn," I said in a soft voice as I passed her.

"Princess."

"Pleasure as always." No doubt, she caught wind of my sarcasm, and I didn't care at all. I never thought myself above anyone before, but the way she followed orders like some sort of machine made me comfortable feeling superior. At least I had a brain of my own.

I swam through the palace entryway, heading as planned straight for the throne room. The first oddity I noticed was the complete lack of peasants. The second was Mother's empty chair. Other than a couple of guards and a mermaid wiping the coral walls, no one else was in the room.

The mermaid stopped cleaning long enough to acknowledge me with a curtsey.

"The throne room is empty today. Strange to see it this way two days in a row. May I ask where my mother is?"

She brushed a ginger strand of hair out of her face, and then gave me a genuine smile. "Good morning, Princess. The queen is just eating her breakfast."

"Is it that early? My internal clock must be off. I thought it was close to noon."

"Nothing's wrong with your ticker, Princess." Her chipper voice brightened my mood, so I beamed back at her. This mermaid, I decided, I liked very much. "Queen Calypso had a late night is all. Seems Princess Fawna is having a rough time after losing her babe. Such a terrible thing, a miscarriage. Tragic loss for the whole kingdom. The queen cleared her schedule for the morning."

I looked toward the stairwell, tempted to fly back outside and call the whole thing off. My sister needed comfort, but Eddie needed protection. As much as I wanted to be there for her, it would have to wait. The wheels were already in motion.

"What's your name?" I asked the maid. "I should know it; I'm ashamed that I don't. You don't look familiar to me. Have you been with us long?"

"Don't you worry your beautiful royal head, Princess. You're always so busy tending to the kingdom.

SINK

You shouldn't take notice of the likes of me."

"Of course I should. You're a citizen of Atargatis, same as me. And one of the more pleasant ones, I might add."

Her cheeks turned rosy, and she curtsied again. "You're too kind, Princess. Since you asked, my name is Bridget. I've only just taken this position a few months ago, so you haven't seen me as much as you think."

Strange. Mother had a tendency to be very picky about those she allowed in the palace. This woman must've passed months of rigorous scrutiny to gain her position, yet I couldn't recall hearing any talk of a new palace servant being vetted.

She seemed harmless enough, though, so I placed a hand on her shoulder. "You're doing a fabulous job, Bridget. Good to have you on board. I'm so pleased to have met you."

"The pleasure is all mine, Princess Pauline."

"I hope to see you again, my friend."

She curtsied again, and I allowed the indulgence without a fuss. Though I didn't particularly care for the gesture, to refuse it could be taken as disrespect.

The guards paid me no mind as I wandered into the dining hall to find Mother, who was poised at the table with bloodshot eyes. A bowl of diced clams sat in front of her, untouched.

"Something is wrong," I stated louder than intended.

The queen startled, and then glared at me. "Must you sneak up on me?"

"That wasn't my intention, I apologize. What's

the matter with Fawna?"

Mother steepled her fingers below her chin and considered my question. "An infection, I think. From the birth. Must have gone to her brain because she's acting like a dolt."

"You mean she's feverish."

"Not that kind of an infection, child. She's gone mad, I think. When you have a merling, sometimes your body changes in a way that can't be reversed. Fawna is... lethargic at best, depressed at worst. The girl can't even drag herself out of bed."

"It isn't from the birth," I insisted. "It's because you took her merling."

"Fawna knows the ways and reasons. She was prepared for the possibility."

I shook my head, refusing to buy into her reasoning. "There is no way to prepare for something like what she has gone through."

"When I wish to solicit advice from a merling, I will summon for you. Until then— "

"I'm not a merling anymore, Mother. I'm sixteen."

She stood quickly, and swam to my side even faster, pointing a bony finger in my face. "Just because you're sixteen does not mean you understand anything at all. You have a lot of life to live before you can begin to understand half of what you think you know."

The heat of her fury smacked me in the face, and I shrank back. The queen loomed over me, daring me with her glower to argue. This was the part where I was supposed to cower. She expected me to take it all back—to concede that she was right about everything.

Not today.

I breathed in, filling my lungs with enough oxygen to supply my upcoming tirade. Just as I tasted a slew of insults on my tongue, the door to the dining hall swung open.

Prawn barreled in, tripping over her tail, with Jewel in tow. "Your majesty, we have an urgent matter requiring your order."

"Well, out with it then."

"There has been a human sighting to the south."

"I heard no ships in distress."

"Neither have I, ma'am. However, this merling insists she saw them. They could have drifted from out of range. Should I send out a scout before rounding up the mermaids?"

Mother waved Jewel forward, watching her close for any sign of deception. My best friend's face didn't falter even once.

"How did you come about these humans? I'm certain you didn't break the law and go near land."

Jewel shook her head. "Of course not, Your Majesty. My tail isn't big enough to make that distance, anyway. At least not in one day. I went for a swim with the dolphins. The shadow of their lifeboat caught my eye."

"Their lifeboat," Mother repeated. "I don't suppose you noticed their condition. Alive or dead?"

"Alive, my queen. Two males."

I crossed my fingers behind my back, praying to Poseidon she didn't look to me for any sort of confirmation of her reliability. An inward tremble almost collapsed me when Mother said, "Thank you for coming straight to us, Jewel."

"Just doing my duty," Jewel responded with a smile so sweet even I almost believed the tale she just told.

"Go find a safe place to hide until we've collected our visitor. You know how rambunctious our mermaids can get when they've found new friends."

Jewel shot me a subtle look of victory before exiting.

"Prawn," Mother shouted, bringing her first in command to attention. "There's no sense risking it by bringing only a few mermaids. We may leave behind the one with the matching song. Bring them all, just in case."

"Yes, Your Majesty." Prawn swooped around, following Jewel out the door to stir her hive.

"You might take a lesson from you friend, Pauline. There's no question at all where her allegiance lies. Speaking of which, why are you still here?"

I shook off my shiver, and then cleared the gargle in my throat. "There's something I haven't told you. Something about the last hunt."

Mother tsked. "Keeping secrets from your queen. What's next for you, my dear daughter? Planning a mutiny, no doubt."

"It's only that... I was afraid you might react harshly."

"I don't know what you mean. Sensibility is my strongest suit." She snickered a little. Good to know even she knew she was out of her mind. "Perhaps not. Tell me anyway. We'll see whose head will roll today."

"It's about Prawn. When we approached the sinking ship, we found a man with one of those floating things around his neck."

"A life jacket."

"Yes, that. Anyway, he was still alive when we got to him."

"The man you killed. Prawn said you handled that well. I haven't told you how proud I am of that, by the way. You showed greater strength than I gave you credit for."

I chased back a shudder. The last thing I wanted was to hear those words. If she found something to feel proud of me for, I should be ashamed of it.

"But I didn't sing. None of the mermaids did. Prawn ordered his death before anyone had a chance to see if the ocean chose him."

"I'm certain she had a reason."

"Or maybe she's allowed the rush of death to consume her. Isn't that possible? Her judgement might not be reliable if her mind is clouded with blood."

"It's possible," my mother admitted. "I've witnessed it before. If you're right, she could be a danger to the whole kingdom."

"And a danger to you."

Mother flipped toward the door, and then swung back around. "Why come to me with this?"

I bit the inside of my cheek, focusing on the pain instead of the jitter in my core. I was no expert at lying, not the way Fawna was. "If you don't get what you need... you'll die. You're my mother. No one wants to watch their mother suffer. Not even you, I suspect."

She dropped our eye contact and moved her gaze to the floor. "I didn't let her suffer, Pauline."

Heat burned in my throat again. Scalding words threatened to coast out, but I swallowed them down. She believed her words, and, for all I knew, they could be true in the physical sense. A simple beheading wouldn't yield much pain. What she didn't understand—what she wasn't capable of understanding—was that when the sword slicing through someone was held by their own daughter, the devastation would be insurmountable. I couldn't imagine even death could end it.

"I'm sure you had no other choice." The lie tasted vile.

Quiet settled between us until she dashed out, grabbing my arm. "You come with me. We'll confront Prawn together."

She dragged me through the throne room doors and into the entryway before I managed to wrench my arm free. This wasn't the plan. I had to get in the dungeon without her knowing or all this would be for nothing. It wasn't supposed to go this way, and I couldn't allow it to.

"Mother, stop."

Her forehead wrinkled. "You brought this to my attention," she reminded me, puzzled. "I can hardly let her continue leading the hunt when her integrity is in question."

An uncharacteristic on-the-spot idea planted itself on me. A way to put myself, by appearances only, on her side. "Yes, but if she thinks I fixed the doubt in your mind, she will see me as the enemy. As it stands, she views me as your rival. We could use that to our advantage in case she's too far gone."

Mother's cheeks lifted into a proud smile. She placed her hands on my shoulders and squeezed. "Now you're thinking like a royal. Stay here. I'll observe her from a distance. Let's keep this between the two of us, all right?"

My stomach turned at the look of adoration on her face, but I forced a nod.

She twisted toward the open ocean, and then swam straight into the chaos of a dozen mermaids desperate to find their ocean's pick.

As soon as her silhouette disappeared, I took off for the now-empty throne room.

Blood pounded in my ears when I shoved open the heavy iron double doors. They creaked, muffling the sound of my gasp. Poseidon's head was already pushed down. The throne tilted back, exposing the opening to the dungeon.

CHAPTER
11

"What are you doing down here?" Fawna spoke so fast her words jumbled together. I approached her with a slow stride, as if she were a bloodthirsty shark blocking my path. She hid her hands behind her back. The muscles in her arms flexed under the strain of holding something heavy.

The map still sat on the desk. I relaxed a little, knowing my prize hadn't already been claimed. "I could ask you the same thing."

She eyed me, suspicion swirling in her silver irises. "I was fetching something for Mother."

"She couldn't have asked you for anything. I was just with her."

"Yes, I know. I heard the two of you talking about Prawn. If she's deceiving us, I thought there might be a spell down here to help."

"You were going to bring Mother her own spell book?" I pursed my lips. She wasn't getting off that easy. Either I was getting smarter, or she was losing her edge. "Don't you think if there was some kind of truth potion, Mother would have already fed it to the whole clan?"

Fawna brought the book in front of her, fingers

white from clutching it so tight. "Maybe she over-looked something. She said it herself—she isn't great at sorcery."

"And you thought you'd take up the trade. Call me pessimistic, but I don't think she'll be thrilled at the idea. The only one in the kingdom allowed to practice magic is the queen, remember?"

Fawna swished her tail hard in place, casting me a sullen expression. "At least I'm doing something to help. Trying to, at any rate."

"She doesn't need my help."

Half of her lips moved up to a crooked smile, revealing a dimple on her right cheek. "I think you just got her away so you could come down here to steal something."

I thought for a moment, but I couldn't come up with a single reasonable excuse to throw her off. Nervousness stayed at bay, though. Something told me Fawna didn't want her presence here known any more than I did.

"And you took advantage of her absence for the same reason, I suspect."

Her mouth fell to a frown, but she didn't deny it.

"I have an idea," I offered. "Get what you need and leave. I'll do the same. No one was ever here."

"You have got to be kidding me. Now I'm making deals with merlings," she mumbled, more to herself than to me. "Okay, Pauline. Just turn around so I can finish finding some things. You already know one item too many."

My tail made a small loop, circling me in place to face the wall. Fawna huffed, and then grunted as though she picked up something as heavy as the bolder outside my grotto.

"Do you need help?" I asked over my shoulder without looking.

"No, I've got it, but thanks." She breezed past me. I floated up, trying to get a peek over the back of her head. "Don't you dare," she warned, so I retreated back down.

Whatever she took, it sounded big enough for Mother to notice it was missing as soon as she came back down, which gave me an uneasy feeling in my chest. She might notice the map was gone, but likely not until I had enough time to get out of Atargatis, maybe for good.

That was when it hit me hard.

This was the moment of no return. Once I took that map, stealing from Mother, stealing from the kingdom, I could never come home. Going through with this sealed my fate. I would live the rest of my life like Myrtle. An outcast.

School merlings would hear my name and stick out their tongues, the way I had when Ms. Star told us about the nasty old sea witch who dared defy the queen. Mother would make sure my name would be synonymous with a treacherous traitor.

A lump in my throat threatened to be my downfall. My home wasn't perfect, but it was all I had ever known. Some people and things I wouldn't miss at all. It might even feel good to be free of Mother.

I couldn't imagine never seeing Jewel again, though. Never watching her blue hair blend in the ocean, envy rolled in affection gripping me every time it seemed to disappear. My best friend, and even some of the other merlings, I would miss forever.

Without noticing, I had floated toward the dungeon opening. I looked up at the dim light cast down from above, considering. It wasn't too late. Nobody would be the wiser if I just turned around, and I was certain Jewel wouldn't mind a bit.

No. Eddie was worth it. I couldn't live with myself if I didn't give this my best shot, for him. If it didn't work and we lived in some clammy cave for the rest of our lives as pariahs, then at least we'd have each other.

"You might want to hurry up," Fawna suggested. "It isn't going to take Prawn long to talk her way out of the trouble you stirred up for her. She's a good swindler."

"Don't worry about me. By the way, Fawna. I know you're having a hard time dealing with... everything. I've kind of got my hands full for the immediate moment, but once my plate is clear, I'd really like to be there for you if you'd let me."

Fawna stopped swimming, though she didn't turn around. She sniffled, nodded, and then continued her ascent toward the throne room.

I wasted no time swooping up the map, rolling it tightly before hightailing it out of that creepy, musky dungeon. After replacing the queen's throne back to its upright position, along with Poseidon's bald head, I rushed to my grotto.

I kept the map tucked inside my forearm, hiding it as best as I could. The effort appeared needless, though, since there were only a few merlings and their occupied mothers in the square and none at all in the palace.

The guards, and Bridget, all must've joined in the hunt. A little giggle escaped as I imagined their faces, stern and frustrated when they realized they "missed the humans". Jewel sent them on a wild sea turtle hunt.

"I've got it," I screamed as I entered my grotto, waving our salvation over my head.

Eddie sat on my bed with his face in his hands until he heard me. He looked up, dark circles under his eyes and his mouth agape. "Pauline, thank God. I was worried sick. If you weren't back by nightfall, I swear I was coming in after you."

"Why should you be worried?"

"Oh, gee, I don't know. Maybe because you left with your sister, who I think you called evil or treacherous or something, and then didn't come back all night?"

An annoying little flip tickled my stomach. He looked disheveled, as if he had been up all night long concerned over me. I floated to him, took his hand, and said, "Forgive me, Eddie. I stayed in the palace. It didn't seem proper to share my grotto with a... male."

His cheeks flushed pink, but his embarrassment didn't stop him. He pulled me against his torso, wrapping his arms around the small of my back. "I'm glad you're safe," he said into my hair.

The scent of human lingered on the collar of his shirt, mixed with an aroma unique to him. A smell I couldn't place, probably from his world, warmed my core as I breathed it in. Something spicy and exotic.

My hands loitered around his neck longer than they should. His touch was far too intoxicating to let go without a struggle. I forced myself to push away, and then wiggled the map between our bodies.

The electricity between us was nothing more than a trick of the ocean; a spell cast in the interest of continuing my species. It couldn't be allowed to fester and infect my judgement.

Dear Poseidon, it sure felt real, though.

"You're going to want to see this," I said, my voice shaking.

"What have you got?"

"I think I might have found a way to return you home." I unrolled the scroll across my bed.

"Get out of town." He studied it with tense brows, recognition apparent on his face. He pointed to the bottom tip of Florida. "That's where I'm from. Key West."

"Not so far away. If we can get these gills off you, I can swim you there."

His hand rubbed at one of the slits on the side of his neck. "How do you plan on doing that?"

"We're going to visit Myrtle, my aunt. She's a sea witch. A good one, I hear."

"Time out." He made a T symbol with his hands. "You told me to stay away from mermaids in general. Now we're supposed to go find a sea witch? She'll probably zap me to ashes the second she sees me."

"No, no. She's not like that. At least, I don't think she is. I haven't actually met her, but Mother despises her. Apparently, when my mother ordered humans to be killed, Aunt Myrtle stood in protest. She kept interfering, trying to find ways to stop her. Myrtle was banished for it."

"Okay. So she's one of the good guys. You think she's powerful enough to send me back?"

"I don't know," I admitted. "It's worth a shot. Anything is at this point."

"Even if she could..." He waved his hand over the map. "I don't see any place on here that says 'secret good-witch grotto'."

I laughed, effortlessly and full of sincerity. The way he made jokes when others would fret was endearing. In the short time I'd known him, he impressed me with his ability to shrug everything off and tackle the situation at hand. A quality one didn't find often in the ocean.

"This red smudge," I pointed out. "I'm pretty sure that is where she's hidden."

"Pretty sure?"

I lifted my shoulders, and then dropped them in exasperation. "I'm going on a gut instinct. It's all I've got."

Eddie shifted his eyes from the map to me, and then back to the map. "Let's do it."

"Really?" I bounced in place. Finally, actually doing something instead of sitting around wishing for this all to end.

"Yeah. If your gut says swim to the red dot, then that's where we go."

"You're putting an awful lot of faith in me." A pang of worry zapped my shoulders, making me tense up. What if I let him down?

He mimicked my exaggerated shrug, but with a full-blown smile creasing his eyes. "Well, Princess, you're all I've got."

I felt under my bed, pulling out a brown leather satchel. After filling it with the leftover food and stuffing the map inside, I turned to Eddie.

"We should probably wait until its dark. There's a shipwreck a few miles east of the kingdom, outside Mother's jurisdiction. If we can make it there, we'll be in the clear. We'll rest until morning, and then, with any luck, we'll be at Myrtle's by the end of tomorrow."

CHAPTER 12

As night fell and the mermaids inside the kingdom settled in their grottos, Eddie and I made an uneventful exit. I forbade myself from looking back, afraid I might have a change of heart. Leaving behind the comfort of the only life I'd ever known was a terrifying leap. One that chilled me to the bone. The truth was that there was no telling what waited for us in the open waters.

Eddie's trudge was slow and difficult for him. Without a tail, water was a brutal force to fight against. When I asked him why he chose to take steps instead of floating on his belly and propelling himself with his limbs, working with the water instead of against it, he claimed to prefer the feeling of solid ground under his feet. It didn't take long for me to figure out he had no idea how to swim. For the sake of his pride, I let the issue drop.

About halfway to our destination, his labored breathing hit a high point. His face paled and he dropped to the ground, landing on his bottom. He ran a trembling hand through his black hair and shook his head.

"I have to rest," he huffed.

I nodded my understanding. "Of course. You're

breathing like a fish out of water."

"My chest hurts. I feel like my lungs are going to explode."

"You have to steady your breaths. Do it with me." I took one long breath in, and then a slow breath out. Repeating it as he followed my example. Some color returned to his cheeks, that beautiful bronze shade reclaiming his features. When I was certain he had recovered enough, I took his chin in my hand, forcing him to look me in the eye. "Stop being stubborn. It's all right to ask for help."

"I don't need help. It's just, I don't have a tail. You're better fitted for this environment than I am. It'd be like you flapping around on land. You wouldn't get anywhere."

"Eddie, I've met plenty of humans who could traverse the water just fine. You can't swim, and that's okay. You need to let me help you."

"Sure, okay. Let me just climb on your back and ride you like a whale." He laughed at his own joke, but I just planted my fists on my hips.

"That's exactly what you're going to do."

"Ha! That's a good one."

"I'm serious, Eddie. Mermaids are a lot stronger than we look."

Eddie clenched his jaw and looked away. "I can't do that, Pauline. I'm the man here. I don't take piggy-back rides from princesses."

"Good Poseidon." I let out an animalistic growl. "You humans are so infuriating. Look, I get that where you come from the women are delicate and you do everything for them, like opening their doors and carrying their purses." I held out my satchel, my way of showing it was *me* carrying the load and not *him*. "Down here, though, it's different. We rule the ocean. Mermaids build the walls, make the rules, and get everything done. Stop being a chauvinistic piece of krill and let me help you."

"I am *not* chauvinistic." His tone was stern, but his mouth twitched, threatening to reveal his amusement. "I'm independent. There's a difference."

"You can't afford to be independent in the ocean. Surviving down here means working together. You help me where I lack, and I'll do the same for you."

"Sounds like a good deal. Except, you're still not carrying me. That's too far out of my comfort zone. I'll walk."

"You're either going to kill yourself from exhaustion or it's going to take us two days to get there instead of two hours."

"We better get moving then. I'm pretty anxious to see which it'll be." Eddie winked at me, and the burning anger creeping up the back of my neck receded in an instant.

I chewed on my lip, mumbling some pretty ugly words under my breath as he laughed. "Fine," I said. "I have an idea."

I pinched my thumb and index finger together, pressed them against my lips, and blew. A loud, high-pitched whistle sliced through the water. A second later, I blew again, and then a third time.

He cocked his head, watching me with furrowed brows. "What're you doing?"

"Calling us a ride."

"What—like a taxi?"

"What's a taxi?"

"You know, big yellow car with a horrible driver inside who can't speak English."

"A car? Oh, wait. I think I've heard of that. It has four wheels, moves by itself?"

"That's it."

"I'll never understand why you don't just walk where you need to go. It seems unhealthy to live so sedentary."

"Not everything is close by. Sometimes, the supermarket is like, ten miles away.

"So, you build things within walking distance. There isn't anything we need outside swimming range."

"Then what about this ride you're calling? Must've used it before to know about it."

I shook my head, searching the ocean for a sign of movement. "I've never used him for travel, just for fun."

"Whoa, whoa. Him?"

An eruption of bubbles in the distance caught my eye, and a flutter of excitement burst in my chest. I waved at the shiny grey blob. Realizing it was me, the dolphin whistled and clicked so eloquently one might mistake it for chatter.

He swam right into me, sending me backward with his weight. I grabbed his dorsal fin, and he spun us in dizzy circles as I hugged him. When I finally let go, the seafloor wobbled. Eddie's outline swayed from side to side, and then settled straight once I regained my balance.

"Um." Eddie's jaw hung open as he looked over my dolphin friend, half-fearful, half-dumbstruck. "What. Is. That?"

Somehow, even clueless looked good on him. "This is Mort. He's my friend."

"He's a dolphin."

"Sure. Come on, you can't tell me humans are only friends with other humans."

"I guess you can count dogs and cats. Well, dogs anyway. Cats don't care if you're there or not as long as there's food in their bowl."

"Are dogs a kind of fish?"

"No. Dogs are furry and slobbery and just plain happy to be alive."

"Mort is happy, too. See how he smiles?" Mort opened his mouth and bobbed his head, confirming my observation. "He's wonderful."

Eddie rubbed the back of his neck as he approached the dolphin with his other hand held out. "I guess any friend of Pauline's is a friend of mine. Put 'er there, Mort."

I looked at Mort, blinking. "I have no idea," I told him, but Mort knew what to do. He set his flipper in Eddie's open hand, then they moved their appendages up and down in tandem.

"Good job, Mort," Eddie praised. "It's called a handshake. Just a polite way of greeting one another or saying farewell, that's all."

"Strange. I wonder how Mort knew what to do."

"He spends half his time in my world and the other half in yours. I bet he's picked up all kinds of gestures from both. So, what's the plan?"

"Hold on to his fin," I ordered with a smirk. "And don't let go."

"You want me to ride him?"

"It's him or me, Eddie."

He huffed out a line of air bubbles and grumbled, "Fine." His hands closed around Mort's slippery flesh.

"Are you gripping tight enough? He's going to go pretty fast."

Eddie nodded. "I'm good."

"All right. I'll be right behind you." I clicked and squeaked at Mort, instructing him where we needed to go, and he took off like a silverfish getting chased by a great white.

Eddie's yowl trailed behind them. Just for show, Mort flew up to the surface, leaping out of the water and into the air, then crashed back down. My tail burned from the strength it took to keep up, but it was worth it when I caught a glimpse of Eddie's face.

Exhilaration peeled his mouth back into a splendid smile. His blue eyes almost glowed, putting the color of the ocean to shame. He hollered and shouted in celebration, taking in every ounce of adrenaline and steering it away from fear and toward pleasure. Every adventure life had to offer him, he seized and used to better his enjoyment of circumstance.

Eddie wasn't just a survivor; he was an adapter. Life threw fire at him, and he collected it to make a torch to bring him through the dark. Any doubt I had about the path I was on disappeared in this moment. He deserved to live, and as long as I was breathing, no harm would come to him.

As fast as we traveled, it only took about five

minutes to get to the shipwreck. Mort put Eddie down, docile and gentle. Eddie threw a fist in the air before patting his new friend on the nose.

"That was awesome, Mort. Come see me when I get these gills off. I owe you a big ol' fish for that ride."

Mort thrashed his head up and down, as if he understood every word.

"Thanks, buddy," I said, petting his underbelly.

He left us alone at the foot of the wreck. Eddie examined the beaten vessel. Holes the size of entire reefs decorated the starboard side. Barnacles and salt crust stuck all over. Tiny fish that had claimed this as their home darted in and out, busy to finish up the day.

He banged on the side of it, and then winced at the metallic vibrations his impact set off. Little bits of rust peeled off, and then floated to the seafloor. "This is where we're spending the night?"

"Unless you've got any better place to hide." I ducked in one of the larger holes, making my way inside.

Eddie's clunky footsteps followed. They echoed off the barren structure. It was picked clean. Every useful item, from the captain's chair to the anchor, had already been ransacked most likely minutes after the ship reached its resting place. I didn't remember this particular ship sinking. Judging by the style and materials used to build it, it was only just a few years older than I was.

"Jasmine and I used to play here all the time."

"Creepy hangout." Eddie stuck out his tongue.

"Weren't you worried about sharks? Seems like a prime location for them to set up base."

"Sharks don't come this close to the kingdom. Unless Mother invites them, of course. They come, they eat, and they leave."

"I hope you're sure about that." Eddie took the satchel from my hands, setting it on the floor before he sat down. "Speaking of eating, I'm starved. Want a sushi roll?"

"A what?"

"A sushi roll. Remember, I made them back in your room."

"Oh, your sister's recipe. I'm good, thanks. No offense, but human food doesn't sound too appetizing. We just don't mix the vegetables and fish here. It's one or the other."

"C'mon." He held out a piece of his concoction. "I flew around with Mort. It's your turn to try something new."

I stuck my nose in the air away from him, but in the corner of my eye, I caught sight of him waggling his eyebrows at me, trying to lure me in. I couldn't help laughing at how ridiculous he appeared with pouting lips.

"You look as though you're trying to seduce me with rolled-up fish." I snatched the food from his hand.

A smug smile spread across his face, chasing tingles up my spine. "Where I come from, we call it swagger."

"This is going to taste foul, I know it."

"Here." He reached over and pinched my nose

closed between his fingers. "This might help."

"Stop that!" My voice sounded nasal and clogged, and he chuckled at the sound. I swatted his hand away, sniffing in a breath. "Are you trying to suffocate me or feed me?"

"You have a mouth, Princess."

"Which I can't breathe out of if I'm eating," I pointed out.

He shook his head, amusement written all over his face. "You sound like such a child. Just try it."

"Fine." *One. Two. Three.* I tossed the foreign food in my mouth with my eyes squeezed shut, and then chewed. The flavors melded together, creating an explosion of delicious. Salt from the nori blended with the sweetness of the shrimp. A soft moan left my lips, prompting my hand to slap over my mouth in embarrassment.

My eyes flew open, finding Eddie's fuzzy face just a breath away from me. Heat from his pink lips traveled to mine. A twinge of electricity drew me closer.

"Did you enjoy it?" he asked, his ego overflowing into his tone.

"It was putrid," I lied. My heart pounded in my ears. His closeness sucked the air from my lungs until I was almost helpless against pulling him into me, stealing the precious oxygen back.

Move away, I told myself, but my body wouldn't budge.

Before I could regain control, Eddie made the decision for us. He cupped the back of my head with his hand, bringing me the rest of the way. Our lips collided, and it was as if a white cap slammed into my chest.

A hunger unlike one I had ever known took over. Like a starving shark, I clawed at his shirt, desperate to get closer and feel his body against mine. He groaned, the sound feeding the beast within.

He kissed me harder, with more passion and less caution behind it. "Eddie," I whispered as he pulled away to trail his lips along the tender skin of my neck.

"Don't worry," he assured me as he nuzzled. "No mer-babies. I just couldn't resist kissing you anymore. I've wanted to do that since the first time I saw you in the life raft. This time, I'm going to remember it, though."

Eddie pulled away, clearing his throat and recapturing his composure. My tail didn't want to work. Ragged breaths left my throat as I panted for air. The realization that I wished he hadn't stopped terrified me, leaving me shivering in place.

"Are you cold?" he asked as he wrapped an arm around my shoulders.

"I, uh..." I stuttered, searching for a way to deflect the attention from my ridiculous reaction to one simple kiss. "I'm fine. Honest, I just... I got a chill. It's drafty in here."

His jaw flexed, and I could tell he was holding back a laugh. "We're underwater. It's always drafty."

My cheeks burned with humiliation. I pressed my palms against them, trying to transfer the heat. "You've got me there."

A moment of silence passed before Eddie mercifully changed the subject. "So, your long-lost aunt. I bet you're nervous."

"Yeah, I guess."

"She's going to love you."

"You can't be sure of that."

He winked at me, tempting me right back into my heightened state just as my body had started to calm down. "Sure I can," he insisted. "You got your level head from someone. I'm willing to bet she's a lot like you."

"I'm not sure where you'd get that from. She's a rebel, a nonconformist. I've spent my life following the rules while she made a lifestyle out of breaking them."

"It's pretty obvious you are willing to bend the rules when the cause is great enough." He held out his hands, gesturing to himself. "I mean, if you were a total drone, we wouldn't be sitting here."

"I suppose that's true."

"My guess is you got just enough of her bad-girl attitude to serve you when it's important. You aren't going to stir the pot just to watch what surfaces when it's settled again. You're a warrior, Pauline. Causing trouble for the sake of it isn't your style, but you can't sit back and watch a wrong."

I squirmed, unaccustomed to the attention and encouragement. Individuality wasn't a trait encouraged by the queen. "You seem to think you know a lot about me," I said as I shifted.

Eddie leaned close again. "The ocean told me all your secrets."

"The ocean is full of tricks, isn't she?" I tsked. "She sends a handsome stranger sinking to the bottom of her depths just to shake things up. Then makes a mermaid think she's fallen for him in the blink of an eye."

"Maybe this handsome stranger and the beautiful mermaid are supposed to shake things up for everyone. *Together*. Just maybe, the mermaid feels so smitten because the ocean has intertwined their destinies, chosen their paths for them. And maybe, this mystery guy feels the same connection."

I bit my lip, fighting back the urge to take every word and bask in it. The thought of Eddie and I being predestined to be together was a tempting idea to cling to, but it wasn't feasible.

Even if we somehow found a way to keep him alive, he still didn't belong here. He had a family—a mother, a grandfather, and a sister. If they adored him the way I did, and I was certain they did, they would want him back more than anything. It would be selfish of me to keep him for myself.

"You speak a lovely proposition." I sighed heavily. "There might even be some truth to your words. My destiny is to return you to your world, not to have you forever."

"Forever is a long time. It's also very far away. Neither of us knows what's in store tomorrow. Who knows? Forever might surprise you."

"You're an optimistic type of sailor, aren't you?"

"Not a sailor. I'm a fisherman. A very tired fisherman." He lay down, patting the ground beside him. "Come on. We've got a big day ahead of us."

I curled up next to him, obedient to his request, not out of habit this time, but out of desire. My body demanded his closeness, and while I was able, I wouldn't deny the longing. His heat layered over me, chasing away any terrible thoughts or fears about what was to come. He draped an arm over my torso to pull me closer, and I let him without protest.

My lashes weighed down until I couldn't keep my eyes open any longer. "Eddie?" I asked with sleepiness in my voice.

"Hm?"

"Why are you being so kind to me? It's my fault you're here to begin with."

Eddie gripped me even tighter. "It's nature's fault, not yours. You're saving my life, Pauline. Whatever happens, we're in this together."

CHAPTER 13

"Pauline."

Eddie's whisper broke through my sleep, webbing itself into a dream of us together, basking in the hot sun on one the human beaches. I had legs, long ones tanned to the same copper shade as Eddie's. We were carefree and laughing; there was no evil queen after us. Nothing but sun and good company.

Paradise didn't visit long.

"Pauline, wake up."

It wasn't until he jostled me that I realized his voice was real. I rubbed the sleep from my eyes and groaned. "What?"

"I hear something."

"Don't be such a coquina."

"I don't even know what that means."

"You know." I yawned. "They bury themselves in sand because they're scared of even the light."

"That's not funny. There's something out there."

"It's probably just a school of fish or a strong current. Go back to sleep."

"Pauline, I'm seri— "

Just as I was about to throw him out of the boat, something slammed into the side, shaking the entire thing. I sprang up, adrenaline spiking. "What in Poseidon's name..."

Eddie's eyes were the size of saucers. He took hold of a low-hanging beam to brace himself. "I told you. It was chewing on the boat! I heard his teeth grinding. Must be a shark."

I peeked my head out one of the smaller holes. "It can't be a shark. We're too close to Atargatis." The tip of a distinguishable grey, flat head disappeared under me. My face went numb as the blood drained to my limbs, preparing for flight.

"What is it?"

I gulped, turning to him. "It's a shark."

"Right again. Score two for the human, zero for the mermaid."

"Settle down. He'll hear us."

"Duh, Pauline. He knows we're here. It's just trying to find a way in."

"This doesn't make any sense. Mother has a protection spell surrounding the kingdom. He shouldn't be able to—"

The hammerhead rammed the boat again, tipping it on its side—the side I was looking out of. I fell face-first, screaming as a loose shard of glass sliced through my arm.

As the vessel rolled, the ocean came alive with the sound of crumbling gears and dislodging screws. Metal clanged on metal. My arms covered my face on instinct, taking the brunt of the debris.

Eddie managed to hold tight. He swung from what was now the ceiling with one arm. "Watch out," he shouted. "I can't hold on much longer."

I started to uncover my eyes, but a blow to the stomach caused the air to career from my chest. My rib cage screamed in pain so loud I almost didn't realize I was yelling, too. Eddie had my face in his hands, but the agony diluted the words coming from his mouth. A sickness roiled in my stomach, threatening to come up all over him. Any attempt I made to shove him off was refused.

A few hard coughs and my lungs began to work again. Oxygen trickled in, and, a few minutes later, my thoughts collected themselves. Eddie still hovered over me, brushing black strands out of my face and telling me to breathe.

"What in the ocean hit me?" I asked, slow and slurred.

Eddie closed one eye and pinched his face together. "It was kind of me. I landed on you."

"Thanks for that."

"I thought the water would slow me down and I'd be able to maneuver over a bit. I'm really sorry. Honest, I didn't mean to."

"I know that, Eddie. Next time, just try to aim better. No offense, but I'd prefer not to break your fall again."

I sat up, and then screeched like a baby seal getting eaten alive. A burn erupted in my torso. The flesh was already turning purple. Eddie pressed his finger just under my breast, against my first rib, and then ran it down each one. When he got to the sixth, I tried to punch him.

"At least one is broken," he assessed. "It's hard to tell with you swinging at me."

I took in a shallowed breath, and then hissed. "I'm going to guess more. Let's leave it at that."

Eddie offered his hand to help me up, and I accepted it. "Can you swim?" he asked.

"I'll be fine. We have a bigger problem, anyway."

"What's that?"

"We're trapped." I waved my arms around like a lunatic. "That stupid trespassing shark knocked us over on the only side with an opening large enough for us to fit through."

"That's good. What that means is he's out there and we're in here. Safe, for now. Until he decides to flip us again."

"What if he doesn't?" My skin went clammy. Shock pummeled into me, sending me reeling in panic. "Eddie, we could be stuck here. We've only got enough food for a couple of days at best. If that shark gives up and leave us here, we're as good as dead."

"So we die at the teeth of a shark or with hungry bellies. I know which death I'd pick."

"This isn't a joke. We could die here, Eddie!"

He took me by the shoulders, steadying me and making me look at him. "Calm down. Pauline, look at me. We're not going to die here. I promise you, I'll figure something out. The wood of the hull is pretty shabby. It would take some work, but I can bust it out if I have to."

"Yeah. Okay." I swiped sweaty hands on my tail. "We'll be all right."

"I know you're hurt, but don't go into shock on me. I need you here."

SINK

"I'm here, I'm here. I just needed a freak-out minute, that's all."

"Good. Now that the freak-out minute is over, I need to wrap your ribs."

I arched a brow at him and inched away. "You're not medically trained."

"You don't know that."

"So, you know what you're doing?"

"Well, I'm no doctor. I've taken biology, though. Plus, I'm a scout. They teach us first aid in case someone gets hurt on a campout."

His strange words jumbled in my head. *Doctor. Biology. Scout.* I didn't know what in Poseidon he was talking about, nor did I care. This time, I was in too much pain to be curious.

"Do you know how to set the bones or not?" I pinched the bridge of my nose, warding off the mounting annoyance with his terminology.

"I think so. "

"He thinks so." I guffawed. "You're not coming near me with an 'I think so'."

"By this time tomorrow, if I don't wrap it, your torso will be so swollen you won't be able to move. You'll let me if you want to make it to Aunt what's her name."

"Myrtle," I said between clenched teeth. "Her name is Aunt Myrtle. Fine. Do what you need to do. Just do it quick."

Eddie took off his shirt, his stomach muscles flexing as he pulled it over his head. Somehow, even underwater, my mouth went dry at the sight. His bronze complexion extended to the rest of him.

Deep grooved muscles in his abdomen made mine tighten—a reflex that sent a searing pain through the rest of my body.

"Hold still," he ordered with a gruff voice. "I won't lie to you. This is going to hurt."

"Thanks for the warning." I held my breath, whimpering as he wrapped his shirt around my tender rib cage. When he pulled it tighter, I yelped a pitiful sound.

"You're a tough cookie, Pauline. I'd be in tears right about now."

I let go of a shaky breath when he moved his hands away. "I don't feel so tough."

He leaned in, kissing my swathed stomach with tender lips. "All better."

Even through the pain, he found a way to make me smile. "Thanks, Eddie," I said softly.

"Anytime. Now, let's figure a way out of here, shall we?"

"There's a porthole over there. You think you can break it? We might be able to squeeze through."

He studied it, and then shook his head. "It's made out of acrylic glass. I might be able to if I had something to hit it with. Trying to punch it out would just break my hand."

"Don't do that. We'd be in real trouble, then."

The boat shifted from under us again. This time, Eddie flew to me, pinning me between his chest and the wall. He gripped the ledge over a porthole above my head. I swaddled my arms around his bare back to hold him tight against me. The protectiveness of his gesture drowned out the sting of his weight against my midsection.

The boat teetered. We both tensed. One loud, heart-rattling creak sounded, and we knew we were rolling again. Eddie and I braced ourselves as the floor flipped over our heads. We dangled upside down, tangled together in a cocoon.

While the impact wasn't without discomfort, we were prepared this time. Instead of flying about the cabin, Eddie kept his hold. A few loose pieces of wood and plaster smacked him, cutting up his back and my hands. Other than a few more bumps and bruises, we managed this tumble unscathed.

We rushed to slide down the wall, righting our direction as we landed. The exit exposed itself to us as a blistering hole in the ship's side even wider now than when we came in. As happy as I was to have a way out, it also meant that shark now had a way in.

Eddie stepped between the opening and me, blocking me with an outstretched arm. "Stay back."

"Are you out of your mind? We need to hightail it."

The creases beside his eyes grew tight and his throat bobbed. "Can't swim, remember? And you're in no condition to carry me this time."

"Damn it." He was right. I wasn't even sure if I could swim fast enough on my own as much as I hurt. "Well, you can't fight off a shark, Eddie. He'll rip you to shreds."

"I know that. I'm going to distract him. When he comes after me, you head for the exit. I'll hold him off as long as I can."

"Stop it."

"Pauline, I'm serious."

"I didn't risk everything to leave you to get eaten anyway. There's no way in—" A soft knock from somewhere above pinged, rattling the disintegrating walls around us.

Eddie stepped back, looking toward the ceiling. "What was that?"

A second knock. A third. Then silence.

I gasped as I shoved Eddie out of the way. "It's Mort!"

"Wait, Pauline, stop," Eddie shouted after me, but I dashed out of the boat without a speck of fear floating in my veins. Mort and I had a code that spoke in threes.

A grey blur rounded the boat just as I got outside. "Mort," I screamed, and then I heard his whistle. I could've fallen to the seafloor with relief when he bounded down on me from above. He tapped his nose against my face, as if checking over my injuries.

"I'm all right, Mort." I laughed as he blew bubbles in my face. "Thanks to you."

Eddie scowled from the doorway, a disapproving grimace on his face. "You should've let me make sure it was clear."

"It is clear," I assured him. "Mort drove that nasty hammerhead away. Didn't you, buddy?"

"You could've been wrong. What if it was just a coincidence? That noise could've been anything."

"It wasn't. Just be glad we're okay. Since when are you so serious, anyway?"

Eddie stalked over to me. He took my hand in his, and then pulled my arm out straight. "Look at this," he said, pointing to the gash. "You're bleeding from head to toe *and* you've got broken ribs."

"But I'm *alive*, Eddie."

"You're not all right. Not even close. If something happens to me, that's one thing, but I don't even want to think about you... I should've done a better job protecting you."

I drew him close and kissed him, soft and sweet, yet still full of meaning. "You can't protect me, not down here. There are too many dangers to watch for them all."

His face stayed hard, filled to the top of his hair with determination. "I'm going to give it my best shot."

CHAPTER 14

"This is it?" Eddie examined the large-mouthed cave in front of us.

Plain and unimpressive, this hovel reminded me of something a simple octopus or squid might inhabit. Whenever I imagined the dwelling of the most infamous sea witch in the ocean, I always pictured a grand, dark castle—one that put Mother's to shame.

Although large, this cave lacked any sort of opulence. Dull black rock formed a natural opening. There was nothing magical or mystic about it at all. However, the more I thought about it, the more it made sense.

Myrtle was supposed to be withdrawn and reclusive. A sparkling fortress in the middle of the ocean that screamed *look at me* was probably not her style. If any of what I knew of her held true, she would prefer something more conspicuous. Something like a modest cave created from simple origins.

"Definitely," I stated with confidence. "It's got Myrtle written all over it."

"You want me to go in first? Scope the place out?"

"I think maybe I should go in alone. Just at first. Explain who I am and our situation."

Eddie shook his head side to side. "No way. Forget it."

"She's my aunt. What are you so afraid of?"

"Pauline, you know nothing about this woman. She's been living by herself for ages. That much time alone does things to the brain. It can make you crazy. For all you know, she's been surviving by feasting on little lost mermaids."

I pressed my lips into a hard line to stifle a giggle. "You sound delusional."

"It's not *that* farfetched."

"Okay, say you're right. She's waiting in there for me to come in so she can gobble me up tail first. What are you going to do about it? She's a *witch*, Eddie. Full of magic. You may be bursting with muscles, but that won't do you much good if she drops you before you even land a punch."

"You know, you're not— "

"Oh, for the love of Poseidon." A grainy, breathy voice came from inside the cave. "Don't you know it's rude to loiter outside someone's home while gossiping about them?"

Eddie and I looked at one another, blinking.

"Well, don't just stand there," the woman said. "Come in if you are. Otherwise, keep on moving."

Without realizing it, I slipped my hand inside Eddie's. My fingers curled around his, seeking comfort as we made our way closer to the woman who was my kin.

"Myrtle?" I asked in a timid voice.

A thin, bony woman with hair as black as mine met us just inside the cave. Brown eyes watched me with disinterest, the exact same shade as the girl in Mother's cauldron. The similarities with her sister ended there. A modest crystal crown tangled in her hair, hanging by a strand. As far as her features, they favored my own for the most part. She had my dimpled chin and soft cheekbones with an almost pudgy face.

Myrtle arched a brow at me, casting suspicion in waves. "That depends who is asking."

"Of course." I curtsied out of habit. "This is my friend, Eddie. He's a... well, you can see what he is. And I'm—"

"Those eyes," she mused, moving closer to study my face. "They're a beautiful shade of violet. So is your tail."

I blushed. "Thank you."

"I've only known one mermaid in the whole ocean to have eyes that color."

Since I had never met her, she couldn't have been referring to me. Yet, I'd never even heard of another mermaid with such unusual coloring. "May I ask who that was?"

She looked away then, as if a painful memory yanked her down into herself. "My mother. She's been gone a long time."

"I know, and I'm sorry. She suffered a terrible fate."

"What do you know of it?"

"Many things I almost wish I didn't. It's a heavy burden to carry, knowing what the queen did to her."

Myrtle turned to me again. This time, her chest puffed out in defense. "Who are you?" she demanded. "Nobody alive today witnessed what happened, with the exception of Calypso and me."

I swallowed hard. Eddie squeezed my hand, urging me to continue. "I'm Pauline. Queen Calypso is my mother."

She snickered, sarcastic and condescending. "Oh, so I have a princess on my doorstep, do I? Forgive me if I don't bow to you, dear. Bad tail and all." Myrtle rolled her eyes, and then headed deeper in the cave.

"I wouldn't ever ask you to bow," I insisted, following close behind her. "Truth be told, I hate the gesture."

"I find that hard to believe considering how keen your mother is on it. When we were children, she would throw a fit if a peasant didn't greet her just the right way."

"That sounds like her."

"Strange to see a human and a mermaid traveling together. Forgive me for saying it, but you both look terrible."

"It's a long story," Eddie explained. "Sharks, ships, a dolphin. Long one."

Myrtle released a long, drawn-out sigh. "I don't get visitors often, and, in general, I prefer it that way. Company almost always brings trouble along with them."

"I'm afraid we're no different," I admitted.

"As much as I would love to throw you out of here, the way your mother did to me, I suppose it would be rude of me to turn away injured wanderers."

Eddie hissed. "That's almost kind of you, thank

you."

Stacks made up of dozens of books littered the cave floor. A leaky cauldron just like the one Mother kept in the dungeon sat out in the open, decorating the very center of the room. The liquid inside boiled pink instead of green, letting off a fragrant aroma that soothed me down to my soul.

I breathed it in. "What is that smell? It's divine."

"Lavender," Eddie answered. "It's supposed to help you relax."

"Indeed it does." Myrtle dipped a finger in the concoction and patted some behind her ears. "One of my favorite luxuries from the human world, so I made some myself. Not all magic has to destroy something, after all."

Dark magic, the kind Mother favored, was never used for indulgences. None other than power, anyway. If light magic was capable of bettering, even in such a small way as getting the smell of saltwater out of my nose, maybe I wouldn't swear it off.

Unlike the dungeon hiding the queen's magic, this room didn't fill me with an urge to run and hide. No ominous cloud chased me around the room, whispering *danger* in my ear. This place felt normal, without the bad vibrations that polluted Mother's castle from top to concealed bottom.

"Speaking of your mother," Myrtle said. "You might want to return her snack to her quick. She tends to get ornery when she has to wait. But then, you know that."

"Her snack?"

She pinched Eddie's cheek, leaving behind a

pink welt from her long nails. "She's still sacrificing humans, I'm sure. Too bad, this one's pretty cute."

Eddie rubbed the skin on his cheek. "That's kind of why we're here."

"I've got to tell you, kid. Your choice in company could use a little upgrade."

The insult sent a jolt of anger into my chest. I waved a finger at her. "Now wait just a minute."

"Personally," she added. "I find the crown-wearing types to be a little high maintenance, but that's just me."

"I'm not wearing a crown, am I? You are, though. In fact, you wouldn't even be standing if it weren't for the magic in the crown you speak so ill of."

She ignored me, patting Eddie on the shoulder. "Don't misunderstand me—I get it. She's a hot little mermaid. But the whole wanting to kill you thing should be a pretty strong turn off. Oh, oops. Did I spoil the surprise?"

"Stop it," I shouted, smacking my hand down on one of her precious books. The room went silent, and all eyes turned on me. "I'm nothing like my mother, okay? I hate crowns. I hate when commoners grovel at my feet. What she does to humans makes me sick, and I'm doing everything I can think of to stop that from happening to my Eddie."

The tense, mocking muscles around Myrtle's mouth relaxed. For the first time, she looked at me with something other than contempt. Not quite friendliness, more like she was trying to piece me together. A splash of warm trickled down my cheek, and I realized I was crying. I swiped that tear away, hoping she hadn't noticed it yet.

The pity in her eyes told me I wasn't quick enough. "All right." She nodded. "We're at peace then, you and me. I'm sure you can understand my defensiveness toward... *your mother's* kind."

"My mother is a monster."

"We've all got a little bit of monster inside us, Pauline. Some of us are just better at keeping it under control than others."

"Myrtle." Eddie stepped forward, clearing his throat. "We've come to ask you for your help."

"Of course you have. That's the only reason anyone comes to visit."

Shame pierced my heart. What a lonesome life this poor mermaid had endured, and there I came, knocking on her cave with my hands out like a beggar. "If I had known what I do now, I would've chosen your side much sooner. I swear to it."

"Yes, well, we all know what they say about hindsight." She smiled at me, a warm, honest smile that melted the ice between us. "What is it you need?"

"It's going to sound a little strange," I warned.

"In that case, may I?" She reached her hands out, pressing each one on either side of my temple. "I so rarely get to use my magic."

Eddie furrowed his brows, unsure of what she meant. I understood perfectly, though. She asked permission to read my mind. With my limited experience with telepathy, I didn't have any idea how successful she could hope to be. If she was powerful enough, perhaps she could break through my barriers with ease.

If nothing else, she might get a sense of my spirit and see I spoke the truth; that though I shared my mother's blood, I carried none of her ideals in my heart. I nodded my consent, and she closed her eyes.

A rush of heat penetrated my skull, almost scalding my brain. Electricity zapped from her fingers. Every cell in my body came alive. A loud hum bounced from one ear to the next, never leaving my head.

Flashes of memories that weren't my own played like a slideshow. War and death, blood and carnage. Even through the tragedy, an image of my grandmother's face stuck out. Her purple eyes filled me with a debilitating sadness. My mother's rage and Myrtle's remorse flowed through my veins. I saw my aunt's exile, felt the isolation as if it was my own.

Then, outside Myrtle's cave, I watched a young mermaid approach. One with silver hair and eyes. Before she got too close, a wall went up, leaving me with nothing but blackness beyond that point. Myrtle allowed me to see what she wanted me to see, but not anything more.

When my aunt's hands left my head, a rush of energy left my body. I fell back into the waiting arms of Eddie. I turned to face his chest, burying myself in his skin and smell. The back of my eyes burned, but I couldn't tell if it was from tears or a blistering anger I felt regarding Myrtle and all she suffered for standing against my mother.

"You want me to send him back," Myrtle stated, voice gentle. She frowned when I told her I did. "But that's not all you want from me, is it?"

CHAPTER 15

Eddie pressed his chin into the top of my head, trying to get a look at my face for confirmation. "What does she mean?"

I shook my head, refusing to give up my secret. There was no telling how he might look at me if he knew. This was bigger than he was.

Even more than I wanted to save his life, I felt compelled to end this once and for all. Calypso shouldn't get away with taking another human life. I couldn't bring down her reign myself, but with Myrtle's help, we might just stand a chance.

"One problem at a time," I insisted.

Myrtle thought for a moment, running her eyes up me as though she was trying to assess my strength. She wanted to know if I was strong enough to get the job done.

"I'll help you with him." She nodded toward Eddie. "As for the rest... There are some things I need to consider first."

"Of course," I answered.

Eddie ran his hand through his hair, his expression difficult to read. "So, there's a way to send me back, then?"

"If that's what you wish, I can make it so." She

sauntered toward a stack of books, reading the spine of each. "Ah-ha! Here it is. Eddie, be a dear and lift the others off the top. I may look youthful, but I don't feel that way. The crown does wonders for my skin, but not a thing to soothe aching joints and bones, I'm afraid."

Eddie straightened his back and broadened his shoulders. "No problem."

She slipped out a thick, golden book with black letters. *Deformities Inflicted by Way of Magic*, it was called. Myrtle licked her fingertip, and then flipped through the pages. "Let's have a look. Gills, gills, gills. Where are you, gills? Oh, here you are."

"Wait a minute." I covered the page with my hand. "Have you done this spell before?"

"Once or twice. Nothing to it really."

"Who came to you and asked you to perform such a strange kindness? It doesn't seem like the sort of thing many mermaids would risk."

Myrtle narrowed her eyes on me, looking over her slender nose. "Despite what you may believe, you are not the only one on their side."

The words left me gasping for air. They came from her lips, but I heard them in Fawna's voice. My sister said the exact same thing to me in the kitchen. I thought she meant the peasants, but now...

Eddie's fingers brushed my back. "Pauline, what's wrong?"

I licked my lips, wondering how they could be so dry and chapped even underwater. "Nothing. I just remembered something. Aunt Myrtle, since you've done it before, I have to know. It won't hurt him, will it?"

"Oh, yeah," Eddie mumbled. "I hadn't thought about that. How bad is it going to sting?"

She swatted my hand away. "You won't remember a thing. Just like when Pauline put the gills on you to begin with, your mind will enter a meditative state so deep, your subconscious won't feel any pain at all."

"That sounds good to me."

I peeked over Myrtle's shoulder as she scanned the page with a scrawny finger. *Eye of a crab. Ink of a giant squid. Scale of a virgin mermaid.* "That's where you come in," she said with a wink.

My cheeks grew hot. I stopped reading, afraid of what else she'd find to embarrass me with. "It seems pretty simple. All very basic ingredients."

"Except one thing." She marked the page before closing the book. "It calls for the poison from a tentacle of the Irukandji jellyfish."

Eddie leaned against the wall, lost in thought. "I don't' think I've even seen a jellyfish since we've been down here."

"There are plenty around," I warned. "The sting of a box jellyfish is enough to make you wish you *were* drowning, believe me."

Myrtle hummed in agreement. "Box jellyfish are nasty little suckers, for sure. The Irukandji is a type of box jellyfish, but it puts the ones we're used to around here to shame. They're tiny little things, no bigger than my fingernail. Small as they are, they hold one deadly punch of venom."

"You mean they're fatal?"

"They can be. I've seen them kill more than one mermaid in my lifetime."

"I think I watched a documentary about them in science class once," Eddie added. "I guess Australia has a big problem keeping them off their beaches."

Myrtle plopped the book back on top of the stack it came from. "And there's the problem. There aren't any around here. You may find one every blue moon off Florida's coast, but for the most part, they aren't a danger to us."

"Which also means they can't help us." My heart sank to the bottom of my stomach.

"Not necessarily." Myrtle scratched the top of her head, itching out an idea. "Last I heard, there was some talk about farming them. Of course, that was a good bit of time ago. I have no idea if the idea took off."

"Why the hell would they do a thing like that?" Eddie asked. "You just said they were dangerous."

Icy eyes glared at him, telling him to watch his mouth in front of his elder. He took notice, dropped his head in shame, and muttered something like an apology.

"Because," Myrtle started. "The venom also holds many medicinal properties if compounded with the correct materials. It's also, as you see here, used in magic. Any powerful spell requires powerful ingredients."

I nodded. "That makes sense. Mother never mentioned farming any jellyfish or anything else at all. I couldn't see her breeding anything that might encourage sorcery."

"I didn't say it was being done in Atargatis."

"Then where..." I leaned forward, into the revelation I knew she was about to unveil. There were rumors about a rogue clan of mermaids, but Mother swore them to be false. According to her, the most one would find anywhere else in the ocean was a stray mermaid or two who was either lost or exiled, like Myrtle. A breeding operation, especially with a dangerous creature so small, would require a good-sized, organized population.

"There is a whole world outside your kingdom, Pauline."

"Tell me," I insisted. Eddie came close, draping his arm around my shoulders for support.

"In case you faint or something," he explained with a smart smirk. "You have a habit of falling, and this sounds like big news."

I gave him a playful shove, and then turned my attention back to the story.

Myrtle went on, keeping her voice low and slow so I would understand every word. "There is an entire society outside Atargatis. A collection of the outcasts and exiled. Most by force, some by choice. All believe, as you do, that what your mother has done for hundreds of years is barbaric. They could not live under her rule, so they created their own. You know of the kingdom, though not its true purpose, I suspect. I'm sure you've heard it called Atlantis."

My tale wobbled. Eddie held tight. He was right, and that fact fueled such a hatred in me that I thought it might burn right through my heart. Mother said it was dangerous; she said the humans created such a noxious atmosphere for themselves their own earth sank beneath their feet, contaminating the water it landed in.

But it was a lie. It was an outright lie.

Queen Calypso was so afraid of losing even a smidge of power that she was too ashamed to admit there were mermaids out there who could not be bullied into her way of rule. Admitting so many disagreed with her meant admitting she didn't have the control she appeared to.

Instead of confessing the truth to herself, she lied. Not just to any peasant on the street or one of her officers, but to *me*, her flesh and blood. My loyalty through the years meant nothing at all. Knowing that, I was glad to defy her now.

"If there's a kingdom filled with people who believe the way you do..." Eddie began. "Then why do you live here? I should think you'd prefer the company."

"My job is to act as a liaison between societies," she clarified. "As much as I would enjoy living amongst my kind, I'm needed here. Every once in a while, a mermaid like Pauline wanders in, looking for another way of life. It's my job to lead her in the right direction."

"You sacrifice a lot."

"There are many worth sacrificing for. You, for instance, mean enough to my niece to make her turn against her entire way of life. Her whole family. That's pretty special."

Eddie looked at me with a soft expression, as if the entire world stood in front of him. I could've melted at that look. "Pauline is pretty special."

"You're sure this is what you want, boy?" She gave a pointed glance at the spell book.

He opened his mouth, but I cut him off. "Of course this is what he wants. He has a family that is worried sick about him. His mother thinks she's lost her son. Besides, it's not safe for him here."

I couldn't look at him. Truth was, I didn't want to know if he agreed with me or not. If Myrtle asked what *I* wanted, I wouldn't be able to hide the fact I wanted him to stay. However, this wasn't about me. It was about what was right for Eddie, and I couldn't risk that the ocean's trick of attraction would make him choose to stay.

"Very well then," Myrtle breathed, face solemn. "You'll have to make the trip to Atlantis." She made her way to a vanity on the other end of the room, opened a drawer, and pulled out a pendant. "They aren't warm toward outsiders. Especially royals. It isn't that they're excluding, they're just skittish, you see. I'm sure you can understand."

"I do," I answered. "I imagine the royal family has caused them all much heartache."

She held out the golden medallion, shining and polished with an engraving of a plump half-octopus, half-human figure on it. "Wear this."

"Man," Eddie marveled. "That looks just like Ursula."

"A friend of yours?" Myrtle asked. "I'm surprised there would be a creature such as this on land."

"No, no. From *The Little Mermaid*. The wicked sea witch."

Myrtle and I blinked at each other, and then I shrugged.

"My sister made me watch that movie over and over when she was little."

"This isn't a movie," Myrtle warned, as if she knew what a *movie* was. "This medallion is a symbol to the merfolk of Atlantis that you're on their side. That you mean no harm to them."

I slipped the chain over my head. "I'll protect it with my life. What do you say, Eddie? You said you wanted to go Atlantis."

"I'm game." He shrugged. That same mysterious face made a reappearance, and I decided I didn't like that face one bit. I preferred to know what he was thinking. "How do we get there?"

"The same way you got here," Myrtle replied.

I took the map from my satchel, unrolling it to show her. "I took this from Mother's collection. Atlantis isn't on here."

"Sure it is."

"No, look. The only things on here are a few human landmarks, Atargatis and this big red spot, which is you."

She pointed at a grey smear—one that looked like someone accidently got squid ink on the side of their hand and swiped it there.

"That's just a smudge," I argued.

"That's what your mother wishes it was." She jabbed her finger into the map. "That is Atlantis."

I turned the piece of paper, orienting our direction and figuring the best route. "That's not far at all. Come on, Eddie. The sooner we get the jelly, the better."

Myrtle stopped me in my tracks. She lifted my chin with a finger, making me look her in the eyes. "A word of warning to you, Princess Pauline. You are about to dive into a world you never knew existed. Everything you think you know will be toppled on its head. Your very sense of being will be shaken to the core. Are you prepared for that?"

"I've been dropped on my head more than a couple of times these last few days." I winked at Eddie. "What's a few more bumps?"

She slanted closer to whisper in my ear. "I don't know if what your heart wishes most can come true. The only thing I can promise you, dear, is that at the end of this, no matter how it turns out, your beautiful and pure little heart will be in pieces."

CHAPTER 16

Out of the kindness of her heart, Myrtle cast a spell on a team of orcas to pull us in a home-made basket large enough for two to Atlantis. Neither Eddie nor I were in any condition to make the trip on tail or foot. Before leaving, she gave me some ointment for my ribs, instructed me to apply it twice a day to speed up bone reformation.

Eddie, she claimed, was hopeless. If he hadn't learned to swim by now, he wouldn't ever, she said. I refused to accept her assessment, vowing to teach him one day. First, we had to get those gills off and get him home.

We arrived just before sundown, yet even in the dusk, Atlantis was a place unlike any I had ever seen. Human homes still stood in their places, though some were falling to shambles. The mermaids had roped them off, restricting access to presumably prevent further damage.

Castles built from gold glistened in the distance. So many of them lined the streets and circled the square. There must've been a castle for every mer-maid, with some to spare. A high, slotted gate that shimmered encircled the whole city, closing it off from the evils of the ocean.

Eddie whistled, and then clicked his tongue. "Fancy place."

"This is what a kingdom should look like," I said. "The wealth is spread out. There's enough gold for everyone."

"If this is how the commoners live, I can't imagine what the queen's castle looks like."

The orcas carried us to the entrance of the gate. As soon as we stepped out of our carriage, the magic wore off. Both of them looked at us with dazed, confused eyes. Before I could explain what had happened or make sure they recovered well enough, they swam away without a proper goodbye. We were left on our own with only Eddie's clumsy feet and my tail to find our way back. I simmered for a minute, thinking about their lack of manners. They were intelligent enough to know they should at least say hello.

The door in front of us was gigantic. The miniscule slit between it and the wall revealed an almost-invisible deadbolt in the center. *The unlocking mechanism must be on the inside*, I thought.

"Should we knock?" Eddie asked. "We could just swim over the top. Well, you could. Then you could let me in."

"I suppose the former would be the most polite. We should watch ourselves. Remember what Myrtle said about how they feel about outsiders."

Eddie banged three times with his fist, hard enough to send a clanging vibration out into the water. Silence filled the air for a moment, but then we heard a click as the bolt slid inside the door. A figure emerged as the door swung open, slow and methodically. The mermaid on the other end wanted to see us before we saw her.

A green tail showed first, followed by a firm, chiseled torso not even a mermaid like Prawn could hope to achieve. As the shadow the door cast pulled back, I noticed one important article that wasn't to be found—this mermaid had no clamshell bra. Nor did she need one, since she had no breasts. Firm, pronounced pectoral muscles much like Eddie's took their place.

"What do you want?" The stranger's voice was deep, gruff, and not at all mermaid.

"Eddie..." I clawed at his arm as the realization of who was on the inside washed over me. He shushed me, babbling on about how I should calm down and not make a scene.

He didn't understand. On the other side of that door stood the one creature I grew up believing didn't exist. The one reason our lives went on the way they had. Necessity made us kill Gene, Mother said. She said there was no other alternative.

Yet, here in front of me, was proof all those humans had died for no reason. A merman. Alive and talking, just a few steps away. A sickness slammed into me, one I couldn't shake with a simple breath or two.

"Is she all right?" the Atlantian asked, and I could've laughed at the question.

"You're a merman," I stuttered.

The new creature opened the entrance the rest of the way, a quizzical look on his pale, freckled face.

Blond stubble blended with the skin on his chin. He rubbed at it with rough, worn knuckles. "You act like you've never seen a merman before."

"How could you... You're not supposed to exist. Mermen are extinct. "

He held his arms out wide. A sly smile spread across his face. "Yet, here I am."

I poked at his rib cage, needing to feel physical proof this was not an illusion—that I hadn't hit my head when that ship flipped over so hard that I was now either unconscious and dreaming or completely mad.

Iron hands slammed down on my shoulders as Eddie yanked me back. "You're acting like a lunatic," he warned. "He's going to send us away."

The merman ignored Eddie, laughing. To my discomfort, his attention was fixed on me only. "You truly believed we were gone."

"It's what my mother told me," I admitted, sheepish and feeling like a dolt. "It's what everyone told me."

"I apologize. It was rude of me to laugh. I've been told what it's like in Atargatis. Thank Poseidon I've never had to experience it myself. What's your name?"

"Pauline." Again, out of pure habit, I curtsied. The second I stood upright, I realized my mistake. Only a royal would greet someone in such a manner.

The merman, who only seconds ago presented me with kindness and understanding, turned cold in an instant. His posture went erect. Any hint of kindness on his face hardened into pure disdain.

"You're the princess," he stated.

I nodded. "I am, but—"

"You can tell your queen her magic is no good here. We've constructed a conduit to absorb all black magic. Sending her own daughter was the play of a coward, anyhow. Should she wish to face us herself, she is welcome to try."

He tried to close the door, but Eddie blocked it with his arm. The weight of it could have crushed his bones like a twig, but the merman stopped, as if he didn't have it in him to injure even a perceived intruder.

"My mother didn't send me. Myrtle did. See?" I lifted the pendant from my chest to show him. "I wear the medallion as proof."

The merman's jaw flexed as he studied the image on the gold circle, no doubt inspecting it for some sign of forgery.

"It's real," I insisted.

"How do I know you didn't just steal it?"

Eddie stepped between us, and the merman blanched at the sight of his legs. He was so fixated on my juvenile reaction to seeing a merman for the first time, he seemed to have missed the legs in the room. "A human," he said, stunned.

"That's right," Eddie retorted. "A human. Now I ask you, if Queen Calypso sent her, do you think she'd let her bring me along? No. We both know what she'd do to me if she knew I was down here, and it ain't pretty."

Everything paused for a moment. The ocean went quiet. As suspicious as it was having the princess knock on the rebels' door, the merman realized the truth in his words. He stepped aside to open the path to inside. "Come in. Hurry, before someone sees. The last thing we need is that old wretch thinking we're harboring humans now, too. She'll really bring her wrath down on us."

We did as he asked. Once the door was locked and secure, with us on the inside, Eddie asked, "I thought you said you had a security system in place? You talked about a conduit."

He shrugged, and then waved at us to follow him. "A bit of a bluff. Our energy system dilutes black magic, but it can't destroy it. Enough to give us a running chance, if need be. I'm Dalton, and you are?"

"Eddie. Pauline's human, I guess you could say."

Dalton ran his seaweed-green eyes over me, making me squirm. "The ocean has fated you together. Lucky human, you are."

Eddie grabbed my hip, tugging me close against him as if proving his possession. "What do you mean by that?"

"Nothing aggressive, honest. I'm not chasing after your tail." He winked at me, and it held no effect compared to when Eddie did it. "Just meant you could've ended up with one of the queen's die-hard followers is all."

"Oh." He released his grip a little. "Yeah, I guess you're right about that. I sort of hit the lottery, you could say."

I batted my eyelashes, putting on my most formal tone. "Dalton, may I request an audience with the queen—or king—of Atlantis? I have a matter most urgent to discuss with him or her."

"There is no queen or king here. Atlantis is ruled by the people."

Eddie guffawed, and I pinched him for it. "Then who decides the rules and punishments around here?" he asked.

"We don't exactly have a problem with crime here," Dalton answered, not seeming the least bit offended. "We do have a court of elders who meet to discuss development and the needs of the city."

"Perfect," I squealed. "May I see them?"

"It's getting late. They will meet with you first thing in the morning, I'm sure of it."

We passed by homes more majestic than even Mother's castle. Not a single hovel or hut to be found. Purple coral decorated the whole kingdom, contrasting with the gold of every building in sight. Colorful fish swam about alongside mermaids and mermen. By my count, the population here must've exceeded Atargatis by a hundred, at least. While we had only a few dozen mermaids, most of them living in poverty and squalor, Atlantis managed to maintain many more while ensuring they lived civilized lives.

Everyone smiled and waved, to each other and us. Eddie garnered a few confused glances, but not one of the merfolk seemed appalled at his presence. Curious, maybe, but not disapproving.

"Everyone is so friendly," Eddie marveled aloud as he waved at a group of giggling young mermaids. They seemed impressed with him, and I couldn't blame them one bit. He was the most gorgeous human I'd ever seen, and I doubted they had ever seen one before at all.

"Myrtle said you might not be so welcoming," I said to Dalton.

"You wear the medallion. Plus, he's a human. He bears no threat to us."

"Well, thank you for your hospitality. It's wonderful of you to allow us to enter your sacred space."

"We're sympathetic to the human cause. We've been told what Queen Calypso does, and we are happy to help you hide him."

"I don't want you hide him. Well, beyond tonight, that is."

"Then why bring him here?"

"Myrtle requires an ingredient for a spell. One she hopes you might have here."

Dalton squinted at me. His wall was creeping back up, and I realized what he must be thinking. The princess whose mother bathed in dark magic was searching for a rare ingredient. It couldn't have looked good. "What kind of spell?"

"Only light magic, honest. It isn't for my mother. Myrtle is trying to help me remove Eddie's gills so we may send him home."

"But... you're soul mates. The ocean said it was so. Forgive me, I know your mother is a powerful villain, but she does not control the ocean itself. When a mermaid is tethered to a human, it's for a purpose."

"Hey." Eddie ruffled his hair. "I never thought of it like that."

I shook my head, refusing to entertain the notion. "All those human males my mother suffocated served no purpose other than to continue her tyranny. I *won't* let Eddie share their fate. As long as he's in the ocean, he's in danger."

"You have a noble heart." Dalton took my hand in his, and then brushed the top of it with his lips. The sound of Eddie's teeth grinding was so loud Mother probably heard it across the ocean. "It's an admirable quality, no doubt. Understand, however, that a heart left untended can wither with ease."

"What the hell does that mean?" Eddie snorted, stealing my hand away from the merman.

Dalton smiled at me and said, "She knows."

And I did. I knew what he meant like I knew my own tailfin. When Mother was my age, her heart was broken. Instead of allowing herself to grieve and move on, she clung to the hurt until it blackened her soul. The blackness even shone in her eyes. She refused to mend the cracks, so they became caverns. Had she let her heart heal, things may have turned out very different for her. The kingdom of Atargatis could've been what Atlantis was today.

This merman in front of me, this wise stranger, was offering me a warning. If I wasn't careful, the same thing could happen to me. When Eddie returned to his human world, my heart would be in shambles. I couldn't be too proud to admit I might need someone to help me pick up the pieces.

"I have guest quarters in my castle. You're welcome to stay there for the night, if you wish."

CHAPTER 17

"I'm not sure what you're getting at, Eddie." I sat in front of a yellow vanity speckled with bright emeralds, braiding my hair tight. The mirror reflected back at me, showing the gashes and bruises my journey had left me with. Wincing, I patted one of the cuts with paste made from ground-up sea moss to stop the bleeding.

The accommodations provided by Dalton were more than adequate. He offered us our own rooms, each making my grotto look like a peasant house. Elaborate fixtures and sophisticated art hung from the walls.

Jutted bedrock large enough for my entire family sat in the center. Now that morning had come, I tried to prepare for my audience with the merfolk elders, which was a considerable challenge with Eddie interrupting my every thought.

Despite the kindness shown to us since arriving, Eddie paced the room, concocting stories in his head. "I don't know, Pauline," he whispered. "Maybe that guy was right. Sending me back might not be the best idea. Who knows how much it'll piss the ocean off?"

"He didn't say it was a bad idea. Just that he was

surprised."

"Of course he isn't going to come out and say it."

"If he thought it, why shouldn't he say it?"

"It's pretty obvious that he's sweet on you."

"I beg your pardon?"

"Oh, come on. There's no way you didn't notice the way he looked at you. He's probably got his figures crossed that, once I'm gone, you'll come running back here to him."

I waved him off. "You're being ridiculous."

"I don't think so."

"Eddie, listen to me. You can't stay here. Mother *will* find out you're here and when she does, Gene's death will seem tame compared to what she'll do to you. After all, the way she'll see it, you corrupted her youngest daughter. That crime is befitting of quite the punishment, wouldn't you say?"

His eyebrows lifted, and a playful, seductive smile replaced his frown. He walked toward me, slow and with purpose, as if I was his prey. In one swoop, he lifted me from my chair, cradling me in his arms. I laughed, wrapping my arms around his neck.

"You think I've corrupted you, do you?"

"Quite so," I teased. "You've brought me to the dark side, Eddie. And now, there's no going back."

He sat on the bed, dropping my weight into his lap. "Well then, let me apologize properly." His lips pressed against my cheek, and then left a moist, warm trail along my jawline.

"You're making it very difficult to refuse forgiveness." A burning need started in the pit of my stomach, growing until I felt as if I might burst.

"Good." He breathed the word over my lips, sending goose bumps over my whole body until I shivered. "That means my diabolical plan is working."

I groaned, pulling him the rest of the way. Lust grew heavy in my core; my stomach clenched in a desperate attempt to keep it at bay. Kissing Eddie was so natural, so easy. It felt so right that I was utterly incapable of refusing him. If we spent the rest of our lives locked in this room together, I'd be satisfied.

By the time he pulled away, we were gasping for air. He pressed his forehead against mine, and I felt the muscles in his face contracting. "I could lose myself in you," he admitted.

I let myself melt into him. A nagging voice screamed at me to get a grip. Eddie would be leaving, and the way things were going, he would take my heart with him. Jewel was right. She warned me to keep my distance, but I convinced myself I was in control. It was too late now. At this point, all I could do was take advantage of the time I had to drink in the memories.

"I think I already am," I said with a soft, resigned sigh.

A soft rap at the door drew us out of ourselves. Eddie let me go, and I floated off him. "Come in."

Dalton opened the door, flitting his eyes between Eddie and me. "Am I interrupting?"

"Of course not," I lied. "Good morning, Dalton. Thank you again for opening your home to us."

"It's my pleasure. Having another princess on our

SINK

side will only help our cause." His mouth pinched shut. A startled look came over him, as though he'd just let the catfish out of the net.

I replayed his words over in my mind, and a jolt ran through me when I realized what he said. It was Eddie who responded first. "What do you mean by *another* princess?"

Dalton's face reddened. "Why, Myrtle, of course. She is a princess, after all."

"You're sure that's what you meant?" Eddie moved close, fists planted on his hips.

"Eddie." I pulled on his arm. "Don't be rude. I'm sure Dalton wouldn't lie to us." I didn't believe it, not for one second, but no good could come from calling our host a liar.

"It's all right," Dalton said. "After what Eddie has been through, his suspicion is understandable. I brought you some proper wraps for your ribs."

"There's nothing wrong with my shirt," Eddie insisted. "It's working just fine."

Dalton handed me a stack of folded white cloth, pretending not to hear the human's protest. "I'd be happy to help you put them on."

"Oh, no." Eddie snatched the wraps from my hands and glared at the merman. "Nice try, buddy. I'll help her."

"Eddie," I screeched, appalled by his behavior. "What has gotten into you?"

Dalton flashed a bemused grin. "I'll wait for you outside. The elders are happy to meet with you this morning."

Once he disappeared and closed the door behind

himself, I turned a scowl on Eddie. "You're going to get us thrown out of here!"

"For what?" He threw his arms in the air. "Because I prefer another man *not* dress my girlfriend?"

"Because you're acting like an ass. A jealous, stupid pain in the ass."

He pinched the bridge of his nose, and then nodded. "You're right. I'm acting crazy, but it's just because the thought of you running off with that guy the second I'm above water makes me sick to my stomach."

"Good Poseidon, Eddie." I leaned against him, embracing him with a pardoning growl of frustration. "Didn't you hear with he said yesterday? We're soul mates. Even when you're gone, there's no one else in the ocean who would complete me."

"I guess I don't really like that, either. It's not like I want you to spend the rest of your life alone."

"There's no pleasing you." I gave him a quick kiss, and then held my arms over my head with a hiss of pain. "Hurry up and wrap me, would you?"

He did as I asked, being careful as he unwound his tattered shirt from my torso. The sight of my damages caused the both of us to recoil. No longer was my skin milky white. Alabaster had been replaced by a hideous purple shade almost as dark as the deepest pits of the ocean. Two rib bones protruded, threatening to break through my flesh.

Eddie applied the ointment Myrtle gave me. At first, pain seared from his touch. My body trembled, and I bit my lip to keep from crying out. A metallic taste filled my mouth, but I was glad to have something else to concentrate on. He mumbled something about it smelling like icy hot, but the agony deafened me.

Even while he was still smearing the cream, the discomfort gave way to an icy relief as the magical concoction took effect. I breathed out my relief, and then sucked in as he twisted the fresh wraps around my injuries.

"That's going to take a while to heal," he said, his brows stitched together in concern. "I should've been more careful."

"Mermaids heal much faster than humans. I'll be good as new in a couple of days."

"I hope so."

"Don't beat yourself up." I patted his shoulder, and then teased, "We don't have time for that, anyway. Our audience awaits."

We left the room, and, as promised, Dalton stood waiting just outside the door. We followed him to the streets, the fresh daylight giving us our first good view of Atlantis.

Human-made cobblestone streets lined the landscape like an elaborate labyrinth, all roads leading one place or another. I realized quickly that we should stay close to our guide or risk getting lost.

Dalton pointed out the decaying homes of the ancient bipedal civilization that once lived here. Instead of demolishing them to make way for their own improvements, the Atlantians decided to keep them standing as a tribute to the hard work that gave them the sanctuary they used today. Without their initial efforts, Dalton explained, Atlantis would have no foundation on which to build.

He took us to the square in the center of the city. Unlike Atargatis, where the square served a meeting place to plot our latest abduction, they used it to host festivals in Atlantis. It was also used to showcase their greatest possession, which sat on top of a pillar and was covered in a glass dome.

I knew the relic as soon as we approached it. Dalton watched me with curious eyes, wondering how I might react. He knew its origins, no doubt, and stood back a respectful distance to allow me a moment to piece it together myself.

An enchanted crown, with magic practically oozing out of its diamonds. One so regal and elaborate there could never be another like it in the ocean. Yet, I had seen it before.

"This is my mother's crown," I said, mouth agape. "The one she had when she was a girl."

Dalton nodded. "That's right."

"It was lost to her. She searched for years. How do you have it?"

"It was brought to us by a kind stranger."

Stranger, my tailfin. "Myrtle gave it to you," I said, firm in my belief that had no backing. It was an instinct in my gut, nothing more, but Dalton didn't deny it.

"This crown was created out of purity," he explained. "The intent was to allow a good ruler to maintain a peaceful reign without interruption. No one with a darkened heart can wear it, or they will disintegrate on the spot."

A lump formed in my throat as I imagined Mother in front of me, eyes wide and full of excitement at finding her long-lost crown that was filled with infinite magic. She would put it on without a second thought, then burst into ash and filth.

A wicked thought crossed my mind—one that filled me with shame. I could deliver it to her. Her demise, and the ultimate resurrection of Atargatis, would be my doing. While the temptation was strong, I knew I didn't have it in me. Queen Calypso might be a terrible, awful ruler who had committed many sins, but I couldn't kill my own mother.

I wasn't anything like her.

Eddie leaned closer to it, whistling at the sparkling jewels embedded in its titanium frame. "What good does it do you guys if nobody's wearing it?"

"The immortality it's meant to provide doesn't seem to take hold on any of the merfolk here," Dalton said. "It's tradition to try it on every merling when they're born. We've had no luck as of yet."

I pressed my fingers against the glass case. "It will only work on someone Mother chose as her successor. Right now, that's Angelique. She's the queen's evil little clone."

Dalton pressed his lips together and nodded once. "That explains some things. At any rate, the antique does aide us in some ways. Remember that conduit I told you about? This is it. The crown has a unique ability to absorb black magic, making it far less effective."

"Your security system is a tiara." Eddie shook his head.

I beamed, a small laugh escaping my throat.

"You use the queen's own crown to ward her off? That's brilliant."

"I wasn't sure you'd see the beauty behind it," Dalton admitted with a pleased grin. "Come. The elders are waiting."

CHAPTER 18

Four merfolk sat around an oblong table, observing Eddie and me as if we were the result of a hideous experiment gone wrong. Three mermaids and a merman, all with deep-set lines creased on their foreheads. The merman, I noticed, was much younger than the females. The male gender was still catching up, it seemed.

I cleared my throat, bowing my head. "Thank you for meeting with us."

"None of that," the redheaded mermaid grumbled. "This isn't Atargatis. We won't bow to you, and we ask for the same respect."

Strange definition of respect, but one I could get behind nonetheless. "Of course."

"My name is Eileen. This is Ronald and Yvonne. We know you, Pauline. Yvonne in particular."

I tilted my head toward the mermaid called Yvonne, trying to place her face. A mess of blue curls crowned her cranium. "You're Jewel's aunt," I marveled. "I remember you. Well, sort of. My mother... I mean, the queen banished you. You sabotaged one of her hunts. Caught all the mermaids in a fisherman's net, I heard."

Yvonne's face beamed with pride. "You were just

a tiny thing when I left. No more than four, if I remember right. How is my niece?"

"Talented. So very talented and beautiful. She still has your hair."

"You're still inseparable, I imagine?"

"Oh yeah," Eddie teased. "No secrets between those two. Not even about me."

"Strange to have a princess in the mix." The grey-haired gentleman flicked his fin, interrupting our reunion. He spoke quickly, and I got the distinct impression this guy wasn't one for small talk. "We don't see your sort often. Can't recall ever seeing a human in these walls, either."

"Yes." I nodded. "I recognize the circumstances are strange."

Yvonne twisted a blue curl around her finger, devouring Eddie with her eyes. "To what do we owe the pleasure?" she asked him with a wink.

Eddie smiled back at her, enjoying the attention. "Myrtle said you might be farming Irukandji jellyfish."

"Indeed we have," Eileen confirmed. "It's been a resounding success. Fascinating little creatures— full of vile poison and yet an absolute necessity to modern medical science and sorcery. Quite the contradiction to itself."

"We were hoping you might spare just one," I said. "You see, she's trying to create a potion that can—"

"Send your friend back," Ronald interrupted. All business, this merman. "Dalton has filled us in on your predicament."

Yvonne tsked, wagging a finger from side to side. "Why in the ocean would you want to let this one get away?"

"Excellent question," Eileen concurred. "The ocean so rarely reveals one's soul mate. Seems a shame to waste the bond."

The merman waved across the table, gesturing to his comrades. "I believe I speak for all of us when I say you're both welcome to stay with us, if you wish. We could protect you and your human."

"That's a really nice offer, Pauline." Eddie nudged me, but I floated away from him. I needed distance from his warmth if I was going to think with a clear head.

"It is," I agreed. "A very generous offer. One I cannot accept, I'm afraid. By now, Mother realizes I'm missing. She will search for me, and I can't put you in harm's way any more than I can Eddie."

The merman steepled his fingers, leaning in. "Have you thought about what she will do when you return?"

"There are a great many things she could do. Though, if I return Eddie to land before she finds out he was ever here, I can claim I went on a trip alone. A personal voyage, if you will."

"You underestimate the queen," Eileen said. "She has spies everywhere, you know. We've found many outside our walls searching for weaknesses in our conduit's field."

I took in a breath, steadying my thoughts. It hadn't occurred to me that Mother might have sub-jects outside the kingdom, for espionage or any other purpose. My foolish, childish mind thought she confined her rule to her own territory, and now that someone contradicted that belief out loud, I realized how silly it sounded.

Yvonne tapped the table with her fingernails. "You realize that, in all likelihood, she already knows you're here. Prawn is probably halfway here by now." She shuddered. "Ugly little mermaid. I swear the queen grew her in a dungeon somewhere. Spliced the genetics of a mermaid and a shrimp."

"I've never met this Prawn, but I have to disagree with you," Ronald countered. "If the queen knew Pauline was here, she would be banging on the gates herself already."

"And that's why I can't stay," I offered. "As much as I'd like to accept your offer, it would be a very selfish move. A single mermaid, royalty or not, is no excuse for an all-out war."

Ronald pointed out an open window. "Have a look around, Princess. The people of Atlantis far outnumber those of Atargatis. Granted, your mother's magic is strong, but we would stand a fighting chance if it came to war."

"I didn't mean to insult your capability to defend yourselves," I insisted. "I only meant that the death of even one mermaid, be they Atlantian or from my own clan, is too many. The guilt would stay with me until my dying day."

The room sat silent for a moment. The elders watched each other, no doubt using their telepathy to hold a private conversation. My efforts to tap in were useless. They put up a barricade. With my unevolved skill, there was no hope in breaking through.

A glance at Eddie made me tense. He crossed his arms in front of his chest, refusing to even look at me. My unwillingness to budge on the matter might hurt him, but at least it would keep him safe.

"I admire you." Affection flashed in Eileen's eyes. "You've been given a terrible role model in life, and yet you think of others. That trait is yours and yours alone. You should be proud of yourself."

"You're very kind. All of you."

"We will, of course, grant your request." Ronald wrote a note on a piece of parcel. "I do have one request from you, however."

"Of course. Anything."

He motioned toward Eileen, whose voice turned shaky. "I want you to bring something to your sister."

"Angelique?" I asked. "There is no making peace with her, no matter your offering. She has chosen her side, and it is not in your favor."

"Not Angelique. Fawna."

I straightened my spine. A sudden rush of protectiveness coming over me even took me by surprise. Fawna had been through so much. I dreaded the idea of bringing her into more chaos. "What do you want with Fawna?"

"May I show you?"

A wailing cry pierced my eardrums as we entered Eileen's home. Beautifully decorated in pink and pastels, her style made it clear she lived alone.

Femininity touched every corner of the room. It was almost impossible to imagine a merman living in such a testosterone-strangling environment. We left Eddie with the others, which was a shame because I'd love to see his reaction.

"I didn't expect to see you back so soon." A blonde mermaid not much younger than Eileen emerged from a back room, closing the door behind herself. Perspiration peppered her forehead, and even the surrounding water couldn't whisk it away quick enough.

Noticing me, she forced a smile. "We have a guest. I wish I'd have known you were coming. I'd have freshened up a bit."

"Don't be silly." I waved her off. "You've obviously got your hands full."

"I'm Trina, Eileen's sister."

"It's a pleasure."

Pleading eyes turned to Eileen. "Honestly, I don't think we'll ever get that merling to sleep. He's been crying since you left this morning."

The screech reached a high point, and I shoved my fingers in my ears. Poor Trina's eyes filled with tears of her own. For a moment, I thought she might burst out crying, too.

Eileen motioned for me to follow as she opened the door to the merling's room. I wasn't keen on the prospect of deafening myself more, but I complied. She leaned over his crib, offering him a sea cucumber to chew on. Greedy hands grasped at the vegetable. His cries ceased, replaced by the content cooing of a happy baby.

"I swear..." Eileen shook her head. "That woman knows nothing about merlings."

His eyes lit with curiosity as I brushed his tiny hand with the back of my finger. "He's beautiful," I said. "Is he yours or Trina's?"

"Don't be daft. We're both much too old to have children."

The merling released his prized cucumber, curling his teeny fingers around my knuckle. He tugged hard, bringing it to his mouth to suck on. I laughed, bringing my other hand to rest on the blanket just above his head.

I was about to ask her if they were mer-sitting when I recognized the pattern swaddling the young one. Red plaid. A clone of the blanket my nephew was wrapped in when he was brought to the sharks to die.

No, not a clone. The exact same blanket.

"It's you!" I gasped, snatching him in my arms and cradling him against my chest. Water saltier than the ocean prickled behind my eyes, and, for once, I didn't protest when they flowed down my cheeks like waterfalls.

I had him. In truth, I was never certain I could make good on my promise to Fawna that I would find him, but here he was. Safe and sound in the crook of my elbow, giggling at the stupid gawk on my face.

When I brought him closer to rub noses, he took hold of a lock my hair, yanking on it for dear life. Even when the burn teased my scalp, I couldn't wince. Too much happiness weighed on my heart to focus on any discomfort.

"He remembers you," Eileen said with a tenderness in her voice.

"We never got to meet," I responded, shaking my head.

"Perhaps not face to face, but your spirits have known one another for much longer than either of you have been in this world."

"How... Where did you find him?"

"Myrtle brought him to us. She has a pact with some of the sea creatures—orcas, dolphins, the smarter ones. They help her keep watch for victims of the queen's madness, and, in return, she grants them protection. A monk seal found him, brought him to her, and then she to us. It happens from time to time. Whenever Calypso's magic fails and a male is born, which is more frequently as of late for one reason or another."

"You've had him all this time."

She closed her eyes, and then nodded. "We've tried contacting Fawna to let her know, but since you've left Atargatis, our sources tell us the kingdom is on lockdown."

"Why can't you have your *source* inform her? They're in the kingdom."

"We have," Trina said from the doorway. "The queen won't let anyone near either of your sisters."

I scrunched my nose. "That's strange. Why would she cut the princesses off from their subjects?"

Trina came closer, moving an affectionate gaze over the now-sleeping infant. "We have theories. My personal opinion is she suspects we have one of our own on the inside. Since we do, her mere suspicions could be compromising."

"I wonder if she knows about Eddie."

"To the best we're able to determine, she has no idea," Eileen explained. "She's given no indication that she thinks a human is around. It's likely she thinks you've been abducted for ransom, and she is keeping her other daughter's safe from that same fate."

I snorted. "Not like she'd pay it even if that was the case."

Both women pouted their bottom lips, pity etched across their features. I hated it.

"Besides," I continued. "If she took one look at this place, she'd realize the last thing you guys need is gold. Your streets are paved in it."

Trina laughed, boisterous and loud. I held the merling close to my chest, hoping to muffle the sound. If he woke again, he might start crying, and I wasn't done cuddling him.

"They have gone a little overboard with the yellow stuff, haven't they?"

I winked at her. "Perhaps they should try pink instead."

The mouths of the sisters fell open before they both giggled. "Mermen aren't exactly in plentiful supply." Trina gasped between breaths. "The ones who are around aren't interested in old hags like us. Beauty of that is we can decorate however we wish without interference. Eileen and I, we enjoy pink."

"No need to explain," I assured. "It's better than a drafty grotto colored only by nature's good gifts."

"Nature has many fine presents to offer. This merling being one of them. How a mermaid could look at this face and not melt is beyond me."

She was right. Only a fiend with a heart as dark as my mother's magic-rotted eyes would treat such a beautiful, precious life as though it held no meaning at all. A shudder jolted me as I realized how easy it could have been for her to do the same to me if I were simply born a different gender.

A bubble of fury started somewhere in my core, churning itself into an overwhelming sickness. How many other merlings had suffered the same fate as my little nephew, only to be found by the sharks instead of one of Myrtle's minions?

There was only one way to stop this. The only way to ensure not one more merling or human suffered at the hands of this diabolical, downright insane mermaid.

With Myrtle's help or without it, I had to get my mother off that throne.

When I returned to Atargatis, a bloody revolution would ensue. It couldn't be avoided any longer. Somehow, I had to convince myself to think like her if I hoped to win. Hours, maybe days, of planning were ahead of me, but before I could even consider what to do, I had to get Eddie out of here.

"What did you want from me in exchange for the jellyfish?"

The mermaids took notice of the sudden change in me. As hard I tried to conceal the darkness building inside, it must've shown on my face. Their expressions tensed, and Eileen took my nephew from my arms.

She removed the blanket enveloping his tiny body, and then held it out to me. "I need you to give this to Fawna. Don't tell her where you got it, or anything at all, even if you believe you're alone. We can't risk someone overhearing. She'll know what it means."

CHAPTER 19

"**H**ave you ever thought about coming with me?"

Eddie and I traveled in the middle of the open ocean, somewhere between Atlantis and Myrtle's lair. In spite of the vast space surrounding us, his question boxed me in. The strap of my satchel, holding both food and one of the infamous Irukandji jellyfish contained in a bottle, rubbed against the back of my neck like a noose.

I took a deep breath, tugging at the strap that chafed against my sweating skin. "You're asking me if I've considered living on land?"

"Exactly. You'd be safe there. We could be together."

"I don't even know if that's possible."

"Say it *was* possible. If Myrtle had a way to give you legs instead of that tail and take away your gills like she's going to do for me... "

"It's nonsense. Such magic doesn't exist."

"Just pretend. Would you come with me if I asked you to?"

I pondered his question, trying to imagine walking instead of floating. Of living under heavy air instead of in weightless water. Picturing all the trinkets the humans had given me over the years, I thought about how fascinating it would be to see them in use firsthand. Mother's warnings of their world still nagged at me, though.

"What's it like?" I stopped swimming, taking his hand and squeezing it between my own. "I know what Mother has always told me can't be true. No one as wonderful as you could come from what she described."

He closed an eye, reluctance playing on his vocal cords until they squeaked. "Well, let's go at it this way. What did the queen tell you life on land was like?"

"That blood lined your streets in the name of greed and selfishness. She said wars were fought with such frequency you could faster count the days your nations didn't order death upon each other. You hunt for sport, betray each other for currency. Plagues spread rampant among your excessive population, and your land can no longer support your pollution, which has started to trickle down to our world."

Eddie puffed his cheeks out, pushing the air out as he rubbed his neck. "Well, I sure wish I could tell you she's wrong."

"You mean, the one thing she ever told me the truth about was how terrible the human world is?" Sadness stabbed in my chest. I so wanted every dirty word she said about Eddie's people to be a lie. I *needed* it to be. If she made it up, she had no excuse at all for what she did to the humans. But if it was true...

"I wouldn't call it terrible," he defended. "Sure,

we have our flaws. There's a whole lot we have to work on. A lot of bad guys have made some huge waves that make us all look bad. The race as a whole, though, is more good than evil. We look out for each other. We have family, charities, and orphanages. So many people do a whole lot of good things, and not just for other people. There's this organization called The Humane Society, for example. They spend a lot of time, money, and energy to look out for animals that can't look out for themselves."

"Sounds like our worlds aren't that different. There's the good, there's the bad, and then there's the evil."

Eddie placed his fingertips on my hips, and then shuffled his feet to close the gap between us. My skin pressed against his still-bare chest. I breathed in his spicy scent one more time, closing my eyes at the intoxication.

"As long as I'm with you..." he said. "I don't care which world we're in."

His lips covered mine, pressing down with an aching need. My hands slid up his chest, and then snaked to his neck until my fingers tangled in his thick hair. I devoured his taste, knowing it might be the last time I'd have the chance to enjoy it.

The ocean around me spun. My mind went dizzy, and it took me a minute to realize it wasn't from the kiss. A buzzing in my brain started low, but then grew so loud I slapped my hands over my ears, falling away from Eddie.

He grabbed my shoulders, keeping me upright. "Pauline, what's going on?"

SINK

"I don't know," I answered, breathless. The muscles in my face convulsed until I scrunched my face up. "Something's wrong." The seafloor vibrated under my tail. "Do you feel that?"

Eddie shook his head. "I don't feel anything."

"The ground, it's shaking."

"Maybe you should sit down. My feet are actually on the ground, not just floating above it, and it's not moving. I think it's your head."

White noise beat against my eardrums until a voice, just barely recognizable, forced its way through the static. I shushed Eddie, who drew his eyebrows together as he mouthed the word *what*? Whatever signal had been forged between another mermaid and me crackled, and then was lost. Their attempt at communicating telepathically with me came up short, no doubt due to my lack of skill, not theirs.

I didn't need to hear the words to recognize the panic, though.

"Something's wrong." I threw the satchel into Eddie's stomach. He grabbed at it, opening his mouth to inquire further, but I cut him off. "You need to take this stuff to Myrtle's."

"What? I'm not leaving you here in the middle of the ocean. What did you hear?"

"Nothing. I can't explain it. Someone tried to warn me; that's all I know."

"C'mon. Maybe the message was meant for someone else and you just picked up some other mermaid's conversation."

"No. It was for me. I could feel it. Here, take this,

too." I stuffed my nephew's blanket in the bag. "I'll meet you at Myrtle's later, I promise."

"Pauline, there's no way— "

A gagging odor of rotting fish closed in on us. Eddie pinched his nose shut, but I couldn't move. I shivered as the hair on my arms stood on end. That smell meant one of two things, and neither were pleasant options. Either fisherman just chummed the waters, which meant sharks and hooks, or Prawn was nearby. The powerful swish of a far-off tail created a boom in the waters, and I had my answer.

"Stop arguing," I yelled. "Mother's first officer is close. If she catches you, we're both as good as dead. She won't harm me without orders and risk her head, but she won't hesitate to kill you where you stand. I need you to get these things, especially that blanket, to Myrtle, *now*."

Dark eyes and a flexing jaw revealed his struggle. His instinctive need to protect me, his soul mate, and the logical side that told me I was right, battled one another.

"Fine," he finally relented. "But if I hear a struggle..."

"It doesn't matter what you hear, Eddie. Do you understand me? Everything you have in that bag symbolizes our last hope. Not just for you and me, but for my entire clan."

"What are you talking about, your clan? Pauline, what are you planning to do?"

"There's no time." Prawn's presence crashed into me until I felt her vibrations clear as day. She was close, too close. I shoved Eddie toward a boulder in the distance. "She's almost here. Get behind that rock."

He turned back to me, gracing me with one quick, soft kiss before dashing in the direction I instructed. I held up a finger, judging the currents. By the mercy of Poseidon, it was in our favor. The unmistakable smell of human would be sent away from our approaching enemy instead of straight to her.

Swishing my tail with all the strength I had in me, I propelled myself forward as fast as I could manage. The friction of the water tore into my skin, crashing into my broken ribs with a shooting pain. It didn't slow me; if anything, it urged me forward. Perhaps the ocean would strip away any residual odor that might tie me to Eddie.

I covered a good distance before I caught sight of that sharp nose and salmon-colored tail. She moved slowly, inspecting every inch of coral and seashell in her path. A little glee crept into my chest, creating a dim light in the dark terror that filled my heart. Here she was, tracking me like a shark might stalk a lost sea horse, and it was me who had the advantage.

Prawn hadn't even looked up by the time I flew into her, barreling her back. The scream she let out took that tiny spark inside me and set it ablaze. For once, I had the upper hand.

A mess of pink and black hair twisted together as we tumbled tail over fin. She clutched me tightly, refusing to roll on her own. Sand kicked up behind us in a furious storm of earth and bubbles. I dug my fingers into her scalp and tightened my core, bringing us to a halt.

Strands covered her eyes. She blew at them as she cursed, trying to get the thick locks out of her line of vision. "Watch where you're going, you stupid little—"

"Watch it," I warned.

She stilled at my voice. "Princess?"

I clumped her hair in my hands and yanked it back, putting my face just an inch away from hers so she would have no trouble seeing every detail of my face. "That's right."

"What are you doing out here?"

"Don't act so surprised. You were tracking me. I just found you first is all." I swiped my palms on my tail, brushing off the sand. "You were a close second, though. I'm sure you would've found me in no time."

"No, I mean, what are you *doing* out here? Your mother's been worried sick."

"The queen is concerned with her image, nothing more."

Prawn righted herself, and then pushed back her shoulders once she regained her composure. Even miles away from Atargatis, she was a soldier. I entertained Yvonne's theory that Mother conjured her up in her cauldron and decided it held weight. This mermaid behaved like a puppet with Queen Calypso controlling her strings.

The stubborn automaton lifted her chin at me. "We all thought something had happened to you, Princess Pauline. From the looks of you, I'd say we weren't entirely wrong."

I patted at the cut above my eyebrow. My touch brought no pain, which told me it was starting to heal. "I had a run-in with a shark." I told the truth without a flinch. "He capsized a shipwreck I was sleeping in, and I got stuck."

"That's quite the tale."

I shrugged, showing no sign of guilt. "It's the truth."

"If that's what happened, how are you standing in front of me?"

"A dolphin helped me. You remember my friend, Mort. He heard my plea and rescued me."

"Hm." Prawn rubbed her nose with the back of her hand. "Might I remind you your mother has access to some of the most powerful telepaths in the ocean? Many of her advisors are quite gifted in the area of precognition, as well."

"So? You said yourself Mother had no idea what happened to me. It's pretty clear they aren't *that* powerful or they'd have seen—"

"You're absolutely right. They all failed her. All of them spoke of a magical barrier preventing them from seeing where you were. As you can imagine, that was concerning."

I sighed a little, saying a silent *thank you* to my aunt. Since I had never even tried to cast a spell, the only logical explanation was that Myrtle had cast one for us. She shielded us so Eddie and I might make it to Atlantis without the kingdom's guards on our tails.

"You, of all my mother's friends, know how inept I am at even the most basic mermaid talents. Telepathy has even proven to be too difficult for me." I batted my lashes, playing my innocent dimples without shame. "Tell me, Prawn, do you think *I* would even have a chance at mastering something as complicated as sorcery?"

Her lips peeled back, revealing sharp, menacing teeth. "I don't think you did anything, Princess. Except run away, of course."

I floated backward, suddenly eager to create some space between us. Prawn reached into a sack I didn't realize she was carrying, and then pulled out a bundle of rope. Adrenaline spike in my veins at the sight of it.

"Prawn, I demand to know what you're getting at," I insisted with a trembling voice.

Before I could react, the homely mermaid lurched forward, snatching my wrists in her hands and wrenching them behind my back. I almost cried out, but remembered Eddie would be nearby. If he heard the signs of a fight, he might do something stupid.

"What is the meaning of this?" I commanded. The itchy rope rubbed at the delicate skin of my arms. Wrenching at the knot did nothing but make it tighter, pinching my flesh even more.

"It's time to go home, Princess. I have orders to return you at once."

"I hardly think restraints are necessary."

Prawn threw me on to my stomach, hovering over me until her lips pressed against my ear. "The queen sure does. You're under arrest, Princess Pauline. By order of Her Majesty, Queen Calypso."

With all my strength, I thrashed against her, throwing the back of my head into her ugly, pointed nose. She grunted, falling back just long enough for me to roll over and look at her. My jaw opened, but words wouldn't come out. My mother, *my own mother*, was having me arrested.

Prawn gripped her nose between her hands and cracked the bridge back in place. Water seeped into the corners of her eyes, but she never shed a tear. She sniffled, sucking back in a tiny trickle of blood that threatened to drip out.

"You thought you were slick," she teased. "Going to see that sea witch for help. You made one fatal mistake, though. When you're going to meet with the queen's arch nemesis, you don't go telling your blabbermouth best friend about it."

CHAPTER 20

"You will bow to your queen." Prawn's lean tail smacked into mine, sweeping it out from under me. With my hands tied behind my back, I was helpless to stop her from forcing my face into the sand. Sharp, grainy bits cut into my skin, but it wasn't the pain that caused me to shake like a long piece of kelp caught up in a windstorm.

Mother hovered over me, her eyes even darker than I remembered. A trident was in her right hand, and a glowing ball of light in the other. "You've disappointed me, Pauline," she said, her voice ripe with condemnation.

When I remained silent, Prawn jabbed at my shattered ribs with a bony finger. "Well," she prompted. "What have you got to say for yourself?"

"I regret nothing," I announced through gritted teeth.

A scalding heat accompanied bruising fingers as Mother seized my forearm, lifting me off the ground with a sharp tug that almost took my arm out of the socket. I held back a cry, refusing to give her the pleasure. An orange glow emanated from her hand, and I realized the burning was her magic. Out of control and uninhibited dark magic scorched my flesh.

She let me go just as the smell of singed keratin reached my nose. "Leave us, Prawn."

"Your Majesty," she protested. "Are you certain it's safe? What if Myrtle taught her something to use against you?"

"Anything my sister could've taught this dim-witted girl in a couple of days would be useless against someone as seasoned as I am. Wouldn't you agree?" Daring eyes flitted to her first in command, challenging her to suggest otherwise.

She wouldn't, of course. Implying the queen wasn't strong enough to handle a green sorceress would be suicide. Mother's ego was fragile.

Prawn curtsied, shot me a glare, and then took her leave. "I'll be outside if you need me," she warned before disappearing from the throne room.

"Explain yourself," Mother ordered.

I pressed my lips together, and then shook my head. I heard the resounding slap before I felt its sting. As her palm collided with the side of my face, my head whipped to the side.

"You ungrateful little beast," Mother screamed, borderline hysterical. "Have I not given you everything you could ask for?"

I chuckled, spitting the metallic taste of my blood at her feet. "You mean besides a mother?"

"You were fed, cared for, and looked after."

"By the servants. Not by you. You were my queen, the same as for every other peasant in your kingdom. Only instead of starved of food and gold, I was left ravenous for affection and acceptance."

"As if you know the meaning of suffering."

An image of Eddie flashed in my mind. Losing him would be the hardest battle I ever won, and knowing what it would cost me as I fought for his freedom, there was no question I understood loss and heartache. Every breath I took was one breath closer to losing him. Knowing as much made me want to hold my breath until I was blue in the gills.

"That's right, Mother, I do. You think because your heart was broken one time that you know so much more of heartbreak than anyone else, but you're wrong. There *is* a greater loss than a man you *thought* you knew."

"You speak as though you know anything at all about love. You don't. None of you do, and that's thanks to me. If it weren't for what I have done, mermaids would swim around, picking up the pieces of their broken hearts all over the ocean. At least here, in Atargatis, I can protect my girls from that pain."

"By creating loneliness and despair throughout the city? You take away one loss to replace it with another."

"Everyone here loves me for what I have done. Everyone except you."

"No, Mother, every mermaid in this kingdom fears you for what you've done. Nothing more, nothing less."

Mother's jaw trembled, and, for a moment, I thought she might cry. I knew better, though. Her heart was filled with too much hate and rage to even begin to feel pain.

"You should've stayed with that wretched witch." She hurled the words at me as if she meant to skewer me to the wall with them.

I clucked my tongue at her. "I was headed back to her cave when your first idiot in command arrested me. I'll gladly return, if you prefer."

Her eyes bulged from her head, and her voice went higher than the merling's in Atlantis as she shouted, "You betrayed me for my *sister*. The one woman I hate more than any other creature in the ocean. You ran to her and left me and everything I've given you behind."

"Because what you're doing is wrong!"

"So you thought she could stop me, is that it? I have bad news for you, Princess. Myrtle couldn't stop me three hundred years ago, and she can't stop me now. You chose the wrong side."

"Then let me go, and I'll continue on the wrong side. It's my path to swim."

"Absolutely not. You plotted against me." She pointed at the crown on her head. "Therefore, you have plotted against this throne. Treason is your crime, my dearest daughter, and I will see you tried."

I sighed, feigning exhaustion. "We both know this is going to end in banishment, anyway. Save yourself the aggravation of a trial and sentence me now."

"Exile would be too soft a punishment for what you have done." Queen Calypso lifted my chin with the tip of her trident, the heat in it burning my face. "You want your judgement? Fine, I'll give it to you. I will see you executed, Pauline. Your body will thrash above me as I watch you take your final breath. What's more, every moment of it will be a pleasure for me."

Pins and needles ran over my whole body. My throat went dry, and Mother's figure swayed in front of me. She couldn't mean what she said. It was anger, that was all. Her words were spoken in the heat of the moment. When she came to her senses, she would retract the sentence.

"Mother—"

"Don't *Mother* me. You are to be made an example of. If the mermaids see I'm capable of putting my own daughter to death, not one of them will have the gall to even consider doing what you've done. No one will stand against me, Pauline."

My tail went limp from under me, so I slid to sit on the seafloor. She was serious. I thought about begging, as ashamed as I was to admit even tossing the notion about. Surely if I pleaded for my life, perhaps even in front of the commoners, she would grant me a reprieve. Even in the face of certain death, there was no way I could lower myself so far. Just the thought of throwing myself at her tailfin made me sick with shame.

No, I wouldn't reduce myself in such a way just to live under her villainous reign for the rest of my life.

I floated up again, this time raising myself to look in her face. She would see no fear in my eyes. "Do what you must."

The queen's face deepened its shade of red until it rivaled the purple of my fin. She had anticipated a plea for mercy, and my indifference ate at her like a barnacle leeching on her back just out of reach.

Calypso screamed for Prawn, who rushed in with a spear aimed and ready.

"Take her to the barracks," she ordered, planting herself on her throne.

Prawn snickered as she grazed my midsection with the tip of her blade. The weapon sliced right through the wraps that bound my injuries, revealing the weakness for all to see.

"With pleasure," the officer stated with a cruel grin spread wide. She jabbed the spear at me, not hard enough to break the skin, but with enough force to tell me she would fillet me in an instant if I made a wrong move. "Get going, traitor."

I did as she asked, watching my mother with a content smile until she was out of my line of sight. Even if I died at the hands of this mermaid, I did so with a clean conscience and the satisfaction of knowing I stood up when everyone else sat silent.

Prawn corralled me to the third floor, directing me into a room I'd spent my life trying to forget existed. Not a single drop of light made its way into the prison; it was dark and dreary to keep hope from sneaking up on whomever was unfortunate enough to be confined inside.

Slatted metal bars boxed in cage after cage. She shoved me in the closest one, locking the door with a clank. I pressed my back to the side facing her, slipping my hands in the opening for her to release the bindings still holding my hands together.

"I don't think so, Princess," she said. "You're going to rot in here until the queen orders your pretty little head above water. Until then, you aren't to receive an ounce of comfort. The rope stays on."

Caustic words danced on my tongue. The temptation to tell her off, to point out how pathetic I thought her to be, was strong. The realization that these might be my last words to her kept them in my mouth.

Instead, I tilted my head to the side and looked at her as if she were a mere merling, incapable of making any decisions on her own. "I want you to know, Prawn, that I don't blame you."

She stilled at my confession. The mask of a dictator fell before my eyes, replaced by the face of a mermaid unable to understand my empathy.

"You've known no other life," I pointed out. "From birth, you were selected to serve her. After a lifetime submerged in the darkness, one can't condemn you for emerging a tad tainted."

No words for or against me left her lips. She merely watched, trying to decipher the sympathy I offered. I brought my hands back inside my prison, my way of showing I didn't offer these kind words as a bargaining chip for freedom. Prawn wouldn't let me go; there was nothing I could offer her to change her mind. She didn't know *how* to change it. All I could do was extend my forgiveness, for her peace and my own.

Her eyes shifted to the rope around my wrist, but I swiveled to remove it from her line of vision.

"Go on," I urged. "If you take too long to return, Mother will be cross."

"Don't concern yourself with me, Princess. It's your gills on the line here. I don't want pity from a human sympathizer." She squinted her eyes at me before retreating in the darkness.

When I was certain she was gone, I tugged at the rope again, trying to work the loose end of the string back into the knot to unravel it. A few minutes in, and all I had accomplished was tightening the stupid thing. I sank against the coral wall, lifting my tail and dropping it to the floor. Sharp edges nipped at my skin, especially my bony wrists, but I ignored the pain.

For the first time in days, the darkness and quiet gave me time to think. My eyelids grew heavy, reminding me of how long it had been since I'd had a decent night sleep. I was tired, so tired. Sitting here, alone and waiting for my own death, it would be so easy to give in to the hopelessness threatening to take over.

I closed my eyes, relenting to the exhaustion. I wasn't sure how long I slept—a few minutes or a few hours, it didn't matter. The rest did nothing to energize me. This kind of fatigue went soul deep. A lifetime of fighting who I was, along with days spent fighting to stay who I was, instead of who my mother tried to make me. It all bore into my bones, aching down to the marrow.

A loud clang jolted me awake. I darted to the prison bars, pressing my face against the opening. Red hair glowed in the blackness, and I knew the pale face as soon as she came close enough to make out.

"Bridget?"

The housekeeper, the one I just recently met,

swam forward, swinging a set of keys around her index finger. "Bet you're glad to see me, eh, Princess?"

"You're not supposed to come in here. The queen will—"

"I just had some dusting to do." She flashed an innocent smile and winked. "Oh, look. This lock is filthy."

"But..."

The lock creaked as she slipped the key inside. She pouted her lips and said, "Oops. Now look what I've done. I do believe I've set a prisoner free. Completely on accident, mind you. I'm just so dense sometimes, I swear it."

I swung the door open, the metal groaning, reminding me of the sound the gate at Atlantis made when Dalton let us in. "You're the informant," I whispered. "The one the elders told me about."

Bridget didn't answer. "Let me help you," she insisted as she untied the rope.

The fresh, exposed skin itched as if sea lice had embedded themselves under it. I rubbed at the red, raw marks left behind. The number of scars I'd have by the time this was through would likely outnumber the krill in the ocean.

"That's why I didn't recognize you before," I said. "Not only were you new to the palace, you were a transplant. You haven't worked for my mother long at all, have you?"

"Just a few months. I told you that when we met."

"Wiggling yourself into that position couldn't have been easy. You're either brilliant or stupid."

Pink splashed her cheeks as she shrugged. "Let's

call it brilliant insanity, shall we?"

"That sounds about right. How did you know where to find me?"

"With the fuss you put up while Prawn hauled you up here? I think they heard you on the other side of the ocean. Myrtle sent word you might be in trouble. I've come to get you out and to her cavern."

"You work for Myrtle?"

"I work for the cause. From what I've been told, that puts us on the same side. Yes?"

"That sounds like the type of question to ask someone before you untie them," I teased. "If you side with the Atlantians, you have a friend in me."

"Thought so. The first time I met you, I thought to myself, *I like this girl. She's good merfolk.*"

"Thanks, Bridget. Believe it or not, those were my exact thoughts about you."

"Of course I believe it. I'm a very likeable mermaid. Come on. Let's get you to Myrtle." She tugged on my arm, pulling me further into the room.

I pointed to the door. "Uh, the exit is that way."

"Yeah, if you want to get the both of us speared by Prawn and her instrument of death." She pushed at a piece of square coral in the wall, which was just barely a shade lighter than the living rock surrounding it. "First rule of espionage, my friend. Always prepare for the worst."

CHAPTER 21

"What's he still doing here?" I motioned toward Eddie, who slept on Myrtle's bed. Even in his sleep, worry lines marred his forehead, thick and unrelenting. He clutched my bag against his chest as if it was his last hope of ever seeing me again.

Eileen, Myrtle, and Bridget crowded around her cauldron. They each watched the contents with fierce eyes, but closed mouths. Whatever they concocted, it was almost finished.

"He wouldn't go without saying goodbye to you," Myrtle explained. "The boy loves you, you know."

"Eddie only thinks he loves me because the ocean tells him to."

Eileen wiped her hands on her tail, and then rested them on my shoulders. "I don't think you understand how this works. The ocean only selects a human mate if you are *truly* meant to be together. He loves you not because he's been tricked into it. Eddie adores you because of who you are. Don't dilute that."

"And I love him," I admitted with tears in my eyes. "It's because of my love for him that I must insist he is taken ashore the moment he wakes up."

"Pauline, think this through." Myrtle inched forward.

"It's not safe here. Mother knew where I was but not whom I had with me. At least Jasmine kept some of it to herself. She will come here searching for me, and if she finds him—" I covered my mouth, unable to speak the words.

Boulders drifted to the bottom of my stomach, resting there with a painful thud that took me down with them. Out of agony and exhaustion, I finally collapsed. Burying my face in my hands, I tried to hide my weakness, but it was no use. Shudders wracked my whole body as I sobbed.

A soft voice came from the next room. One I recognized, but did not belong to any of the mermaids surrounding me. "Just breathe, Pauline."

I jumped, snapping my head up to see someone who should not have been there. Fawna came quickly at me, scooping me against her and cradling my head in the crook of her neck as if I were her long-lost merling. Too tired to resist, I held on to her, releasing all my built-up emotion as she brushed my hair with her fingertips.

Fawna whispered her command again, over and over, until I found myself complying. Deep breath in, long breath out.

"She was going to kill me," I told her between ragged breaths. "My own mother planned to haul me above the waves and watch me suffocate."

My sister cooed, "I know. She's wicked."

"How could you even think about doing that to someone you love? Unless..." I sat upright, looking her dead in the eye. "She never did love me, did she?"

Fawna brushed a stray strand of hair from my face. "Queen Calypso lost her ability to love anyone a long time ago. It speaks nothing about you, Pauline, you must remember that."

"She's mad." Eileen's face twisted into a mixture of sympathy and anger. "Completely entrenched in the deep end of the ocean. If she could do something like that to her own daughter, imagine what other evils she is capable of."

Bridget slapped her hand on the edge of the cauldron. "Someone has to stop her."

"We will," Fawna promised, and I was struck by it. "All of us."

I inched away from her, examining her frame. My need to seek comfort in her arms blinded me to what her presence in Myrtle's cave implied. "Wait a minute. What are *you* doing here?"

"Remember back in the palace? I told you that you weren't alone in this fight. Myrtle and I have been planning an uprising for years."

My mouth fell open. "But you let Gene die. I watched you stand by and do nothing while I chased after him. You even looked... happy to see him perish."

"I never intended to meet Gene. The ocean pulled a cruel trick, bringing him into all of this. If we are to be successful, we have to wait until the moment is just right. Unfortunately for Gene, it wasn't time yet. Speaking against his fate would only raise Mother's suspicions, and we couldn't afford that. Not for the greater good."

"No offense, Fawna, but I would do anything to keep Eddie from the queen's clutches. That's why I took off with him."

"You hold great bravery in your heart, little one. Looking back, I wish I had chosen differently. The loss of Gene will weigh on me for the rest of my days in this ocean. All I can do to ease it is do my part to make sure that mermaid can never sentence another human to such a horrible fate."

"How did you come to be involved in this then, if not for Gene?"

Fawna's shoulders rose and fell. "I guess I always sort of felt more at home with the humans Mother dragged down here than with the other mermaids. Something about them fascinated me, even as a merling."

"I remember the trips we used to take together to watch them."

"Until Mother started asking more and more questions. She always knew, I think, somewhere deep down. Then, one day, I asked her where our kingdom's name came from. Did she ever tell you the legend of Atargatis?"

"No. It never came to me to ask about it, I guess."

"Atargatis was the first mermaid. She was a goddess who lived among the humans when she met a man and fell in love with him. He was killed, and she was so overcome with grief that she threw herself into a lake, intending to commit suicide. Her love was so transformative and strong, however, that the gods didn't see fit to allow her to die for it. They changed her body, making her half-human, half-fish."

"That's beautiful."

"Mother used that story as an excuse; she said it was proof that love drives you to behave irrationally, that it made one dumb. I saw it another way. None of us would be here if not for Atargatis. She loved a human with such purity the gods denied her death. Could you imagine what she'd say to Mother if she were here today?"

"I can't think she would be pleased."

"Nor do I. That's why, despite how difficult and painful this journey is, I can't leave it. We owe it to Atargatis to see this through."

"I'm sorry, Fawna. I can't imagine what it must feel like, losing so much. Even if it is for a good cause." I leaped up, remembering the gift Eileen gave me for her. "Did Eddie give you the blanket?"

"The what?"

Floating in silence to Eddie's side, I wiggled the satchel from his hands, careful not to wake him. "Your baby's blanket." I pulled it out, and then handed it to her. "Eileen and the others in Atlantis have kept him safe. When this is over, the two of you can reunite."

Fawna pressed the fabric against her cheek, nuzzling at the scent of her merling. Eileen approached her, rubbing her back with her hand. "He's a strong little one, your son. Full of fight and spirit."

"Thank you," my sister softly said. "All of you. For everything."

"He misses you, too," I assured her. "I could feel it."

She swallowed hard as she gave a sharp nod. "I'll

get him back, I swear it."

"You will. I'll see to that myself. How many of us are there?" I asked, referring to the force against Mother.

Bridget waved her hand across the room. "Counting you? Seven. The only ones missing are Donald and Yvonne."

"That's it? Not quite an army. There aren't others in Atlantis willing to fight?"

She shook her head. "They don't care to get involved any further than taking in refugees. I think they're afraid Queen Calypso will bring her wrath to the city."

"I can't blame them there. All right, so it's just us then. What's the plan?"

"Our sources tell us the queen's magic is weakening. She's not able to wait as long before replenishing her crown's magic with human blood."

"Dark magic is never as strong as light," Myrtle explained. "Soon, she won't be able to maintain it at all."

Fawna tapped her chin. "So, when the crown's magic is at its lowest point, her defenses will be the weakest."

"I think that's now," I offered. "Eddie and I set up camp in a ship just outside the palace, still well within the kingdom's spell boundary. We were attacked by a shark."

"Are you certain you were within Mother's boundaries?"

"I'm positive."

Myrtle's cheeks lifted as she smiled wide. "If

sharks can get in, I bet I could, too."

"Besides," I added. "You see how she has aged as of late. The crown is losing its power. The time to strike is now."

Eileen chewed on her lip. "What would be the harm in waiting a little while longer? The more time that passes, the more depleted of evil energy the queen will be."

"And if another human vessel should sink in the meantime, that means another man's life sacrificed and we start the process all over." I dug my fingers into my hair, pulling on the strands. An uncharacteristic desperation came over me, one I couldn't shake. Pacing did nothing to ease the anxiety.

The sooner we removed the queen from her throne, the better.

"Pauline is right," Fawna offered. "We never know when the ocean will pull in another ship. We can't take that risk. Besides, I want my merling back. I can't wait any longer."

Considering Fawna's options, I saw her with a newfound respect. It would have been so easy now, knowing that her merling was safe and sound in another kingdom, to just disappear to Atlantis and leave this all behind. She could go to her baby and start a new life, one without a murderous queen or convoluted ideals. Fawna could have peace, if she chose it.

Easy, yet not heroic. My sister chose the more difficult option not to make herself a martyr, but to ensure an end to this madness would finally come. We would fight beside each other for the good of the kingdom.

"Then it's decided," Myrtle announced. "We go now, while the force is weakened. On the off chance that I cannot break through, one of you will have to take the crown from her head. It's the only way to remove the magical barrier."

"If we do that..." Fawna said. "Mother will *die*."

"It may very well come to that," Bridgett confirmed.

"Are you prepared for that possibility, Princesses?" Eileen asked, watching us closely for our reactions.

My gills flapped, and I let out a shaky breath. "Of course, I would prefer to avoid such an outcome. She is vile, but she's still my mother."

Eileen blinked. "I understand that. However, the queen will not step down without a fight."

"I know that to be a fact," I promised. "If it should come to it, we will do what's necessary. Isn't that right, Fawna?"

"She left my merling out for dead." Fawna's tail trembled. "Given the opportunity, I would do the same to her."

Myrtle cleared her throat. "Good, then. We're agreed. If we can spare the wretch's life, we will. Otherwise, we do what is required." She swam back to her cauldron, dipped a spoon in the bubbling liquid, and poured it over a bracelet. "Hopefully, this will help keep the situation from turning that direction."

"What is it?" I asked.

She tossed it to me without an explanation. "Put it in your satchel. We'll need it."

Bridget bounded forward, her red curls bouncing about in the water. "When do we leave?"

"You aren't going at all," Myrtle told her. "In case things don't go in our favor today, you are still our eyes and ears on the inside of Atargatis. If your identity is revealed, it will help no one. The rest of us leave at once."

The chipper mermaid couldn't disguise her disappointment as a hint of a frown played on her face. She rebounded quickly, though, offering to wake the human. *My* human.

"No," I insisted, much sharper than I intended. "Let him sleep. Myrtle, please leave Eddie's potion with her. Bridget, when he wakes, I need you to take him to the surface and have him drink it."

Fawna rested a hand on my shoulder. "You don't want to be there to say good-bye? It can wait until after—"

"If we don't win and we die, what will happen to him if he's still here?"

I watched as his chest rose and fell in the rhythmic pattern that came with a deep sleep. It was the coward's way out, I knew as much. Out of the hundreds of excuses I could come up with, the truth was I just couldn't face him. If he asked me to return with him, I wasn't certain I was strong enough to tell him no.

The ache returned to my chest as I swam to his side. While I couldn't handle a tearful farewell, there was no way I could leave him without one final kiss. I leaned in, well aware of my audience, and brushed my lips against his. Saltwater not from the ocean mingled with his taste. My hands trembled as I tousled his black locks for the last time, noticing again the way his bronzed skin matched it, along with how much I loved it.

He was perfect.

Whenever I thought of Eddie, this was how I would picture him. Calm and with a look of innocence. I would keep him tucked away in my heart, my protector against the darkness, for all eternity. He would go on with his human life and leave me far behind, but at least he would be free.

CHAPTER 22

"Are you certain this is the threshold?" Myrtle swam just to the line I pointed out, and then stopped with a jolt.

The palace glistened in the far distance, with the now-mangled sunken boat a couple of hundred yards away. A line of enchanted sea stars separated Mother's kingdom from where we waited.

"Positive," Fawna confirmed. "These stars mark the barrier."

Our aunt crossed her arms in front of herself. "Leave it to my sister to drag perfectly innocent sea creatures into her paranoia. Poor things will never know what it is to live a full life meant for a sea star. You know what will happen if you're wrong about her magic weakening?"

"Yes," I responded. "You'll combust."

Eileen's eyes bugged out as she suggested, "Maybe you should wait here, Myrtle. We can handle things—"

"Isn't this your amulet?" Fawna lifted the circular medallion from my chest, showing it to Myrtle. "It has your crest on it."

"I gave it to Pauline as her ticket into Atlantis."

"Since this belongs to you, won't this trinket disintegrate also if Mother's barrier is up?"

"It holds my essence, so yes. That's a brilliant idea. We can toss the necklace over and see if it reacts."

"It won't," I assured them. "I was wearing it when Prawn arrested me." A shudder ran through me as I pictured the gold exploding around my neck, shredding through my face and chest. If I had known that was a possibility, I would've removed it before sneaking up on Prawn and sent it back with Eddie.

"Good, so we're safe then," Eileen said with a sigh.

Myrtle still nibbled nervously at her bottom lip. "Just indulge me. Toss it across the line."

I huffed, grumbling to myself about the wasted time. Myrtle snapped something about it being her neck on the line, so I did as she asked, throwing it just to the other side. When nothing happened, I raised my arms, palms up to the sky.

"You see? Nothing."

She thanked me with a sheepish grin, and I stepped over the threshold to pick up the necklace. As soon as my foot crossed over the line of starfish, a familiar buzz started in my brain.

I fell forward, pressing my fingers into my ears as far as they would go. Muffled questions came from the mouths of the others as they surrounded me, bending over my body to watch as I convulsed.

"Not again," I cried as the high-pitched ringing got louder.

Fawna mouthed my name over and over, but the louder the sound grew, the less I could concentrate on what she or any of the others said.

"Someone's trying to communicate," I shouted over the noise only I could hear. "They're warning me off."

Myrtle straightened her spine, conjuring up a puff of purple smoke in her hand. She flicked her wrist, transferring the colorful magic to the other side of me. It bred on itself, growing larger as it twirled into a tornado, collecting the debris of something far off and bringing it to us. A mermaid appeared on the inside. As soon as the magic whirlwind dissipated to reveal her, the agonizing sound stopped.

A blue-haired mermaid floated in front of us, mouth agape.

"Jewel," I gasped. "What are you doing here?"

She looked at each of us, eyes wide. "I have no idea."

"I summoned her here," Myrtle explained. "I latched on to the telepathic signal being sent to you and brought the culprit to us."

I ran my eyes along the length of my former best friend, lifting my upper lip in disdain. "*You* were the one making that Poseidon-awful noise?"

"I'm sorry." She twisted her fingers together, swimming back just enough to put some distance between us. "I know my telepathic power is too strong. I'm trying to control it."

"What do you want, Jewel?"

"I... it's just... Your mother."

"Yeah, she's an evil, putrid excuse for a mermaid. We know. What about her?"

"She's tearing the kingdom apart in a rage. The

queen said she'll find you even if she has to bring down a hundred sailors herself to gather enough power."

"That won't be necessary. We're headed to her door as we speak."

Jewel cast a nervous glance at my aunt. "Is this Myrtle? The sea witch?"

"That's right." Myrtle smiled. "Glad to hear my name is still common table talk in Atargatis."

"She's no more a sea witch than Calypso herself," I claimed. "Now, if you'll excuse us, we have a date with the queen."

"Wait, Pauline. I'm sorry. I never would have told them where you were going if— "

I raised a hand, cutting her off. "There's no excuse. I trusted you, and you betrayed me. That's all I need to know."

Fawna blocked my attempt to brush past Jewel. "Stop acting like a merling, Princess."

"What? Me? She's the one who—"

"Who was summoned by the queen and her entire council. Jewel didn't reveal anything. I know because I was there. One of Mother's minions tapped into her mind and read it."

I flitted my eyes between them.

"Honest." Jewel crossed her heart. "It took everything I had to push Eddie out of my mind completely so she wouldn't find him. I wasn't strong enough to hide both."

A ball filled in my throat, and I thought I might cry again until I talked myself out of it. She must've seen it on my face, the moment my heart softened toward her again, because as soon as I felt freshly painted walls slam back down, she pounced on top of me.

Jewel's hands circled my neck as she yanked me against her. I held her back, relishing in how good it felt to have my best friend back. With everything else I was about to lose, relief swelled in my chest at knowing she wouldn't be one of them.

"I'm sorry, Pauline."

"No, no. It's not your fault." I took her by the shoulders and held her out to look at me. "I should've known better. You wouldn't turn me in if you had a choice."

Her fingers dug into my arm as she squeezed, peering at me over her inexplicably long eyelashes. "What are you guys going to do?"

The question smashed reality back into me. This whole confrontation could easily get out of hand, putting every mermaid in our path at risk. It was too late to stop our plan—not that I would if I could. Wheels were in motion, pawns were at play, and I was heading the attack on tail.

But Jewel was not a casualty I could allow.

"You need to get out of here," I told her, leaving no room in my voice for argument. "Things have to change, Jewel. This is bigger than you know. I need you to trust me, okay?"

She blinked at me, and then said, "Sure."

"Sure?" Eileen echoed, scratching her head. "You see two princesses, a sea witch, and an Atlantian marching toward your queen's castle, fists drawn, and you're just going to say sure?"

"I trust Pauline. She's never failed me before. Plus, after the way the queen treated me, I have no affection left for her."

"She showed you her true colors. Ugly, aren't they?"

"Hideous, in fact."

Eileen teased a stray blue hair in front of Jewel's face. "You're Yvonne's niece. The resemblance is incredible."

"You know Aunt Yvonne?"

"Very well. She lives in Atlantis with me."

"I'm glad to hear she's alive and well. When the queen banished her, I thought... Well, I thought the worst." She looked between us. "Where's Eddie?"

Guilt set my nerves aflame, sending heat to my face. I pressed my palms against my cheeks to cool them. "On his way home."

"Oh, Pauline," she fussed, pouting out her bottom lip. "You got too close, didn't you? The pain is written all over those hideous bruises on your face."

I shrugged her off, clearing my throat. "I'll come get you when it's safe. For now, find somewhere secure to hide *away* from the kingdom."

After one last hug, she scurried off. We bolted forward. Our approach was swift and sudden. Water rushed past us, flinging bits of salt and sand in our eyes. Mine watered from the abrasion, blinding me. We were almost on top of the kingdom gate before I realized Prawn stood in front, waving her spear around like a maniac.

"She's going to throw it," Fawna claimed, pointing at the officer standing her guard.

Before I could react, Myrtle gathered a ball of orange in her palm and hurled it at her, setting her ablaze in an instant. Pain and fear melted on her face as magical flames licked at her body. She opened her mouth to scream, but no sound left her throat. The roaring inferno around her stole her voice first, and then drank in the rest of her until there was nothing left but ash.

"No," I screamed as I swam to her remains, sifting through them for a sign of life. "Why would you do that?"

Eileen flicked her tail at me, as if my objection irritated her to no end. "She was about to throw that spear at you. Myrtle did what she had to in order to save your life."

"She was only doing her job. Prawn had no choice; she was made this way by Mother. Any guilt she held was only by the queen's hand."

Myrtle came to me, taking my hand in hers and lifting me from the mess on the seafloor. "She had a choice, Pauline. The same way you did. Fawna and you both took your mother's example and used it as something to fight against, not turn to. That mermaid, she chose to submerge herself in the evil of this kingdom. Unfortunately for her, she chose wrong."

"Myrtle's right," Fawna agreed. "Prawn's malevolence was her own doing. Blaming Mother for her own deeds is one thing, but laying another mermaid's debt on her shoulders is unfair."

I brushed the ash from my hand, examining a fleck as it floated away. *There will be fire in the palace.* Ariana, the little merling in Ms. Star's class, foretold of this. Now I knew why she looked right at me when she told of her vision.

When I glanced up, I caught sight of her peering at me from across the square. Ariana watched me, not with fear, but with expectancy. Whatever today's outcome, that merling already knew it.

"I guess you're right," I conceded, steadying myself. We didn't have time for second-guessing. "Goodbye, Prawn."

"This is only going to get worse," Eileen warned. "Are you sure you have the stomach for it, Princess?"

I swallowed against any uncertainty still lingering. "It's too late to stop now. Let's go."

We dashed through the square, warning every mermaid in sight to take cover. The kingdom was falling, we told them, and it was certainly about to.

Chapter 23

I pulled on the door to the throne room only to find it wouldn't budge. "She must've heard us coming," I grumbled. "It's locked."

"Stand back," Myrtle ordered as she held her hands out in front of her, palms facing the frame.

After leaning back, she hurled her weight forward, sending an invisible shockwave at the castle. The vibrations it set off rattled in my chest. Bits of pine flew everywhere as the door disintegrated from the force. I threw my arm up to cover my face, gritting my teeth against the sting of splinters digging their way into my flesh.

"You might've been a little subtler," Eileen complained, picking slivers of wood from her tail.

Myrtle shrugged. "Sorry. There's a lot of pent-up aggression after all these years."

We swam forward to find Mother perched on her throne, her chin pointed up in defiance. She clutched at her trident, knuckles white from the strain.

"So," she started, staring straight at Fawna and me. "Both of you decided to side with the urchins."

Fawna placed herself in front of me, her silver eyes steaming with contempt. "Better with the lowly urchins than the vicious sharks."

Mother cackled, the sound sending a shiver up my spine. "Check your food chain, dearest. The sharks rule the wild ocean, second only to me."

I pushed back the instinctive submission her very presence commanded. Years of bowing down made it a habit to sit quiet and listen to the madness leaving her tongue without objection. Not this time.

"Even the mightiest great white loses his threat if his teeth have been extracted."

She drew her brows together and cocked her head. "One weakling sea witch and three dimwitted mermaids without a speck of magic hold no threat to me. I have an army of mermaids willing to fight in my name."

"Prawn is gone," I told her, pleasure settling in as her face fell. "She's not coming back. The kingdom has been evacuated. You have no one left to fight for you."

Queen Calypso snapped her neck in Myrtle's direction. Tendons stuck out from her throat as her face reddened so deep I thought she might explode. "You," she seethed. "This is all your doing. My daughters never questioned me before you meddled in my affairs. Now, you've turned them against me."

"No, Calypso," Myrtle responded with a calmness that would impress Poseidon himself. "Fawna and Pauline both sought *me* out. Even through the darkness you brought down on them from the moment they were born, they were able to see the light."

Mother slammed her trident down, the bottom breaking through the floor under her throne. With the hole it left behind, one could see the chamber beneath if they gazed through it. "There is no light, you stupid witch. A lesson I tried to teach you long ago. If you had listened to me then, we could've ruled together. Instead, you acted like a fool. Your exile was your own doing."

"All your banishment did was put me in a position to help the victims of your treachery. Atlantis is not only inhabited, but thriving because of where you put me."

"And yet, they still fear me. Isn't that so?" she asked Eileen, who pressed her lips together and shook her head.

The Atlantian straightened her posture, swimming closer to the queen without the smallest suggestion of obedience. Determination tightened her jaw as it flexed. "We are not afraid of you, Calypso."

"Then why have you not stood against me? Surely, as human sympathizers, you would've tried if you had the gumption to do so."

"We value all life, those of humans *and* mermaids. The existence of our kingdom is no secret. Any who wish to join are welcome to do so. We harbor those who flee your tyranny, and we make no apologies for doing so. If we were afraid, we would turn your people away at the gate."

"But your people will not fight me. You're here alone, are you not?"

"My people believe violence will solve nothing. I promise you, though, they have worked tirelessly at finding an alternative means of removing you from your throne."

"And yet you storm my palace walls like a heretic.

You disagree with them, I take it?"

Eileen locked an arm in Fawna's. "I've witnessed what your barbarous deeds have done to mermaids. It is I who am tasked with taking in the young merlings you deem unworthy of your kingdom. I'll do whatever it takes to see you executed the way you sentenced so many innocent human men."

Mother fanned herself as she pretended to become dizzy with fright. "My own sister would never do such a thing. She doesn't have the stomach for it. Isn't that right, Myrtle?"

"That's enough," Myrtle snapped, refusing to buy into her game. She held her hand out for my satchel. I dug out the bracelet, silver and sparkling with magic, and handed it to her.

Her hand clenched around the piece of jewelry as she held it up. "You'll find many things have changed about me, Calypso, and my aversion to harming another mermaid has long since diminished. I *will* have you put to death if you make it so. You have but one opportunity. Put the trident down and hold out your hand."

Calypso examined the trinket, smirking at the evidently obvious purpose. "You want me to put on a purging bracelet? My dear, you *have* been locked away for far too long."

The seafloor quaked beneath our tails, and the trident glowed a putrid green. She pointed it straight at Myrtle, taking aim. Time seemed to slow to a crawl as she shouted in a language I didn't know. All the light in the trident's base migrated, gathering itself in the pronged tip.

I screamed, "Mother, don't," and launched myself in front of my aunt.

Electricity zapped from the trident to my body. Crippling pain shot from my core out to my arms and down my tail, immobilizing me in an instant. Mother waved the trident, and my body flew in the same direction. I barreled through the air, flipping head over tail until I collided with the sharp coral wall. Bits of shell rained on me as I tumbled to the ground. I groaned, still paralyzed from the electric shock.

Fawna tried to swim to me, but Mother latched on to her with an invisible force, freezing her in place. Though she struggled against the magical bonds, her tail wouldn't budge. She cried out, begging me to answer, but I could only blink at her.

Myrtle gathered another fireball in her hand, providing enough distraction for Eileen to make her way to my side. She threw herself on my body, shielding me from whatever fragments might fly my way as a result of the long overdue dual about to take place.

"Do you really think you can beat me, Myrtle?" Mother snorted like a seahorse. "Remember, it was me who won all those years ago."

A sly smile played on Myrtle's lips. The fireball she conjured illuminated her pale face, shining off her black hair. "There's been one major change since then, Calypso. Something you taught me, actually."

"And what is that?" The queen raised her trident, prepared for a shootout.

"I've learned that sometimes even the good mermaids have to get a little blood on their hands if it means defeating a bloodthirsty tyrant."

I hated the words coming from my aunt's mouth—resented them even. To imply that good could only triumph over evil by reducing itself was a bitter, tired outlook. Mother, on the other hand, beamed at Myrtle's statement.

"Very good," she said. "It only took you a few centuries to figure out."

The fireball in Myrtle's hand pulsed, and her hand shook from the strain it took to keep her magic restrained. Just when the light's center started to crack, she flung the orb toward Calypso, who caught it with her own ray. Orange streaked from Myrtle's palms to the center of the room, where it clashed with the green light stretching from Mother's trident.

Good and evil, dark and light, deadlocked, one no more powerful than the other. The palace shook around us as I lay helpless, still paralyzed. Pins in needles pricked at my fins. Feeling was returning, which meant, with any hope, so would function.

Mother's face clenched as she pushed against Myrtle, but my aunt held strong. A whirlwind of silver and black hair whipped around them, mingling violently as though the strands fought a war of their own.

A low rumble gurgled beneath the palace, causing a rafter to collapse. The flying piece of wood missed Fawna by just a few inches. Her screams of terror drowned out the splintering as it crashed to the ground. Chaos erupted all around us. Mother Nature rebelled against the forces in conflict. She threatened to tear this kingdom down, one piece of coral at a time.

Chunks of coral as sharp as glass rained down on me. It wasn't until one put a huge gash in my tail that I realized my mermaid shield was missing. With my head still immobile, I darted my eyes around the room, searching for Eileen.

I zeroed in on a figure with wiry red hair creeping toward the throne, trying to get behind Mother unnoticed. The base of my tail flicked involuntarily when I saw the Atlantian reaching for Mother's crown. Stretching, I wiggled my tail some more, but I was only able to move the bottom of it. Progress.

Eileen's long fingers seemed to elongate as she got closer. The primal part of me still connected to my clan wanted to scream out, to warn my queen and mother of the fate about to befall her. Suddenly, I was glad I couldn't speak. In that moment, my biological predisposition to protect my own might've very well won out.

Eileen leaned over the top of the throne, only inches away from ending this once and for all. Just as Mother threw her head back to pull for more power, Eileen's fingertips brushed the enchanted masterpiece.

The throne fell from under her, toppling backward as Angelique shot out from the corridor the seat concealed. Made entirely from gold, the throne was a heavy ornament. It flipped on top of Eileen, pinning her under its weight.

Angelique took no notice of the mermaid she just defeated without even trying; her focus was on the fire show in the middle of the room. Sparks shot out from the still-unwavering waves of magic.

The sudden entrance of the princess caused Myrtle to jolt. She lost her footing when her arms moved just centimeters, and Mother's green wickedness singed Myrtle's hair, nearly melting her face.

My hand instinctively flew up, reaching to pull my aunt to safety. Good. *Now if I could just get my torso to work.* I searched the seafloor blindly with my fingers until they found a pointed shard of coral.

Mother twirled her trident in victory. She closed in on Myrtle, pointing the instrument into her neck. "You're just in time, Angelique."

"What's going on?" Angelique asked, marveling at the utter destruction around the room.

"Your sisters have decided to head a mutiny. Isn't that sweet?"

Her face fell when she caught sight of Fawna, still suspended in place. The rest of her color was lost when she saw me, flat on my stomach and unmoving.

"What... what have you done?" She spoke to me, not to Mother, and I despised her for it. That rage fueled me, recovering my nerves and my senses until my body tingled with anticipation.

As soon as Angelique's attention returned to Mother and Myrtle, I pounced. My hand clutched that piece of coral until it bit into my skin. Blood trickled down my arm as I landed on my sister's back. My fist found a clump of hair and pulled until she screeched from the sting. The sharp side of my makeshift weapon dug into the tender skin of her neck.

Mother dropped the trident, turning to me with her mouth open. As much as I itched to slice Angelique's pretty little neck, I restrained myself. "Drop the trident or your prodigy dies," I warned.

A sweet giggle started in Mother's throat, and then transformed into a hysterical laugh filled with madness. "Go ahead," she said. "If you think she means any more to me than you or Fawna, you're sorely mistaken."

"Mother!" Angelique shouted. "She's going to kill me."

"And you'll have died in my honor. Go on, Pauline. Get it over with so I can spill *my* sister's blood next."

Angelique's body went limp in my hands. I softened my grip, my anger for her giving way to pity. It was in that moment, I thought, when Angelique saw what Fawna and I had a long time before. That our mother was a selfish, egotistical creature who would do anything to ensure her own happiness and survival—even sacrifice her own children.

I darted my gaze toward Myrtle, wondering why she didn't take the distraction as a chance to strike. Mother followed my thinking, circling back around just as Myrtle waved her hands over Fawna to release her.

Fawna collapsed to the ground, grabbing at her tail. As she tried to knead out a cramp, Queen Calypso sent another zap of magic in their direction. It missed, though not by much, but she rebounded, latching on to Myrtle with the same invisible force that stopped Fawna to begin with.

Myrtle grasped at her throat, her face turning as red as a roll of nori. Veins popped out on her forehead, and a whistle came from her throat as she fought for air. Fawna charged toward Mother, but Mother used her free hand to send Fawna flying straight into Angelique and me.

One of the humans showed me a rectangular toy with dots, dominoes he called it. He would stand them up just to knock them down and watch them topple, one by one. I imagined that was how we looked to her. Pawns falling one at a time under her power, then she'd let us back up just to have the pleasure of watching us take another tumble.

I covered my eyes, unable to bear the sight of Myrtle's struggle any longer. The trashing slowed, and the less noise I heard, the more my ribs felt like they were caving in. Just as the sound of her tail ceased entirely, a crash pulled me back into the fight.

"Put her down," a familiar voice shouted from the entryway.

Eddie.

Mother gasped the same time I did. "A human," she whispered, dropping her arm and sending Myrtle falling to the floor with a thud. Fawna swam over, and then dragged our aunt back toward us.

Eddie took heavy, determined steps toward Mother. When he appeared in my line of sight, so did Yvonne and Bridget. He held something behind his back, and though I couldn't see it from where I was, the small amount of light in the room glinted off it.

Calypso's face paled. Her hands covered her stomach as she leaned forward, gagging.

"What's happening?" Angelique questioned. "Who *is* that?"

My sister's questions drew the visitors in our direction, Eddie's face relaxing the instant he saw me. I swam to him, throwing my arms around his neck. He brought one hand around to pull me in, and then he kissed my face.

"You thought you could get away from me that easy, did you?"

I pressed my lips against his, stealing just a moment before Mother could intervene. "I never wanted to be rid of you," I promised. "Your safety is all that ever mattered."

"Pauline," Mother snapped. "What is going on here?"

"You look ill, My Queen. Are you sick, or is it just the sight of my human boyfriend that has you queasy?"

"Human *boyfriend*?"

"That's right. Eddie, may I introduce you to my mother, Queen Calypso."

"Terrible to meet you," Eddie said, his voice flat. "I've heard awful things."

Mother's voice crackled. She searched for words, stunned. "You brought a *human* into my palace? When did... how did..."

"You really do look pale," Bridget noted with fake concern sweetening her tone. "Maybe you should lie down."

Queen Calypso pointed at her, tipping in place

as though keeping her balance was a challenge. "You work for *me*, so what are you doing with *him*? And you..." She gestured toward Yvonne. "I banished you years ago."

"Feeling a little woozy, are you, Queen?" Eddie winked at me. "A little lightheadedness is normal, don't worry. At least, that's what the merman over in Atlantis told me."

"What in the ocean are you talking about, you filthy, parasite-infested human?"

Eddie flashed her that tempting smile. He brought his prize out in front him, and Mother fell back at the sight of it. In his hand, he held the crown jewel of Atlantis. The very artifact that kept them safe from the evil queen.

Mother's crown.

"Go ahead," he offered. "Touch it."

She extended a finger, hovering it over the gaudy jewels. Her body stiffened, and then jolted back as the crown zapped her on contact. Calypso rubbed at the spot that smoked, cursing.

"What did you do to my crown?"

"This doesn't belong to you anymore," Bridget explained.

"Of course it does. I lost it centuries ago, but it's still mine!"

Yvonne shook her head. "No, it isn't. This belonged to the old you—the Calypso with love in her heart. You're a different mermaid now. Your darkness even shows in your eyes. This crown was created to keep the evil out, and you, my former queen, are nothing but."

Mother squinted at them, raising her trident to get in one last strike. Eddie pushed me behind him, standing his ground even as she waved the thing his face. As the weapon's glow started, Myrtle slapped the bracelet around Calypso's wrist.

"No." Calypso stared at the trident as the power drained from its tip. "No!"

"You're done." Myrtle glowered, stretching her aching neck to the side.

"You won't get away with this, witch. My subjects will see you aired out for what you've done. Angelique..." Mother turned desperate eyes on her middle daughter. "You'll fight for me. You were always the only one I could depend on."

A tense aura descended as all eyes turned on my sister. A trail of tears floated up from in front of her face, but she shook her head. "It's over, Mother."

"What should we do with her?" Bridget wondered.

Eddie snickered. "I say we treat her like she's treated all my people. An eye for an eye."

"Or we could feed her to the sharks," Fawna offered. "The way she does innocent merlings."

Mother's face went white. She heaved, struggling against Myrtle's iron grip on her arm. "You can't do this. I'm the queen!"

"Not anymore, you're not," Myrtle said, jerking her hard.

"Either punishment sounds fitting to me," Bridget said. "She's earned it, after all."

"No," I interjected. "We aren't going to lower ourselves to her level."

Eddie arched a brow at me. "After everything she's done?"

"That's right. We're better than that. Unlike her, we're capable of mercy."

"What do you suggest, then?" Myrtle asked, frustration evident in her voice. "A slap on the tail before we let her go?"

"Of course not." I swam up to Mother. "She should spend the rest of her natural life inside the prison she created. Your punishment, Mother, will be watching your kingdom ruled by another. You'll be forced to witness your clan thriving, repopulating, and advancing, the way they have in Atlantis. Never again will our people be held back because of their ruler's broken heart."

CHAPTER 24

"So tell me the truth." Eddie placed a comforting hand on Angelique's shoulder. "It kind of sucks not getting the job, huh?"

My sister giggled, swatting him away like an annoying sea lice. "Not at all. I wasn't ready to be queen, anyway."

"Someday," I promised her.

"I'm pretty sure Fawna's next in line. Myrtle will hand the crown down to her."

Eddie hissed through his teeth. "Sounds like you got shafted."

"Pauline, your human is talking again," she teased. "You know how much he annoys me when he opens his mouth."

I hooked my arm in his and rested my head on his shoulder. *My human.* If only it could be so.

Myrtle's coronation went on without a hitch. She accepted the throne, which was rightly hers, with grace. The clan accepted her promises of a better life. We opened the palace garden to the entire kingdom, inviting them all to profit from our prosperity with full tummies.

Watching the clan interact with the mermen of Atlantis was like watching a pod of whales during mating season. Mermaids who never knew mermen even existed threw themselves at their prospective mates, showing no shame in how forward they came off.

"I'm sorry it took me so long to do the right thing." Angelique picked at a strand of her hair, biting her lip.

I hugged her tightly. "You just needed to see what Mother was really like."

"I knew what she was like, Pauline. I just didn't care if it meant I'd get to sit in the big seat one day. It was wrong. When she basically told you to kill me, I realized it wasn't worth it. She had to really lose herself to darkness to get to that point. I don't want to lose myself to the darkness, Pauline."

"No way. I won't let that happen."

"Neither will I," Eddie added.

"You, sir, have no say in the matter," I said, poking at him. "Come on. It's time to get your potion from Myrtle."

"I can't believe you're letting him leave," Angelique said with a sigh. "He makes you so happy."

"Eddie doesn't belong here. There are a lot of adjustments to be made with mermen integrating into our clan and a new queen at the helm. Who knows how smooth that transition is really going to be? He's safest on land."

To my surprise, Eddie nodded. "Yeah, besides, after all this, I kind of miss my mom. I don't think I ever appreciated her so much after meeting yours. No offense."

Angelique gave him a quick hug, and then shoved

him off. "Thanks for all the help, *human*."

"Anytime, *mermaid*." He stuck his tongue out at her, and then laced his fingers with mine.

Together, we swam to the throne room, where Myrtle and Fawna sat in waiting. Eddie and I both bowed to the new queen, but she was quick to protest.

"None of that," she insisted. "We didn't like it in Atlantis, and I don't like it here."

"That'll take some getting used to," I said with a laugh.

Fawna tilted her head toward Eddie. "Myrtle tells me you wish to leave us."

"I've got a family at home. A life I should get back to."

"I understand. How can we repay you for your help? You've done a great deal for this clan."

He brought my hand to his lips, kissing the top of it. "Knowing Pauline is safe is all the thanks I need."

Jellyfish swished around in my stomach as heat found my cheeks. He always knew just what to say to make me blush. I would miss that about him, I decided.

Myrtle cleared her throat. "I wonder, Pauline, have you given any thought to joining him on land?"

"What?" I blinked at her, my lips parting as I gawked.

"I just think it would be a shame to lose your soul mate so quickly. The ocean put you together for a reason. Such a rarity, true love. I'd hate to see it go to waste."

"Is that possible?" Eddie stepped forward, pulling me with him.

"Of course it's possible. If that's what Pauline wants."

I looked around the throne room, still in shambles from the fight. There was so much to rebuild in Atargatis. A mess I made that still needed cleaning. There was no doubt I wanted to follow Eddie, to explore the human world and all its treasures. With so much left to do here, how could I leave?

Myrtle sliced her hand through the air, cutting the thought off in its tracks. "Don't worry about us. You've earned the right to be selfish, Princess. You were destined to bring an end to the madness that gripped Atargatis, and you have."

"The truth is..." I turned to Eddie, memorizing the sparkle in his blue eyes. "I don't think I remember how to even breathe without you. The thought of living the rest of my life and never seeing you again, it breaks me."

"Then come with me," he urged.

Myrtle didn't wait for my response. She swam to Mother's cauldron, which had been brought up from below the throne. "Give me that medallion."

I removed the necklace and placed it in her expecting hand.

A golden liquid cooked this time, and she dipped the chain inside, covering the half-octopus/half-human creature entirely. After it stewed for a moment, she took it back out, shaking off the residual potion.

"There," she said, handing the necklace back to me. "As long as you wear this, you'll be of both the land *and* the sea. When you're in his world, you'll have legs. If you return to the ocean, your tail will re-grow. You can always come home, Pauline. I implore you, live your life. Enjoy it. Love each other. When you're feeling homesick, pay us a visit."

I traced the humanoid figure on the front of the medallion, my hands trembling. My throat dried, and I swallowed hard. "I'll go on one condition. Fawna has to come with me."

"You're insane," my oldest sister claimed, but the infectious smile on her face told me she didn't hate the idea.

"You've always loved the humans, you said so yourself. Besides, I can't do this without you. I need you with me."

"I'm way ahead of you," Myrtle announced as she pulled a matching necklace from her pot of magic. She winked, and then said, "I'm a pretty strong tele-path. I knew Fawna wanted to go up there from the first time I met her."

Fawna paused a moment, and then shook her head. "I can't bring my baby into a new world with nowhere to go, and I won't leave him. I've only just found him again."

"Leave him with us." Myrtle lifted a finger as Fawna opened her mouth to protest. "Only until you've settled in. When you're ready and in a posi-tion to care for him, we'll bring him to you."

I took a deep breath as Fawna accepted the en-chanted piece of jewelry and draped it around her neck.

"That's the last time you get to do that with gills," Eddie teased. Myrtle handed him a vile, and he swallowed its contents in one gulp. "Are you ready to feel dry land?"

Fawna slipped her hand into the one Eddie wasn't holding, and she and I nodded together. We swished our tails as Eddie kicked his feet, sending us up toward the surface and our new home.

We crashed through the white caps. The saltwater clung to our skin as we dragged our bodies up on a beach, collapsing once ashore. Sand stuck to my milky knees when I emerged from the water. Eddie observed my legs, and then smiled at me, stealing the first breath of air I took as a human.